Burning Embers

*and Other Stories of
Marriage, Work, and Family*

by

Charlie Close

To Jenna –

Thank you so much for reading my book. Enjoy!

– Charlie Close 6-18-2009

© 2008 Charlie Close
All Rights Reserved.

Cover illustration © 2008 Mister Reusch
www.misterreusch.com
Cover concept by Kathrine Konetzka-Close

No part of this publication may be reproduced, stored in a retrieval system, or transmitted, in any form or by any means, electronic, mechanical, photocopying, recording, or otherwise, without the written permission of the author.

First published by Dog Ear Publishing
4010 W. 86th Street, Ste H
Indianapolis, IN 46268
www.dogearpublishing.net

dog ear PUBLISHING

ISBN: 978-159858-818-7

This book is printed on acid-free paper.

Printed in the United States of America

Table of Contents

Introduction v
Acknowledgements ix
Journey to Michigan 1
Job Search 19
Charlie's First Day of Work 32
Horse 39
Lightning Drive 44
Liverpool 47
Dunkin' the Barbarian 53
Halloween Party 55
Flowers 63
Blue is a Boy 68
Pronoun Muteness 71
The Game 73
Battles 77
Balance 79
Feelin' the Love 82
My Darling Husband 84
Captain Pants 93
Rush at the DTE 98
Valentine's Day Surprise 112
Blissful Morning 116
Your Big Ass Clogs My Living Room 121
Ladybug Kill, Kill, Kill 127
Love and Hug Therapy 132
Rejection...again 136

Burning Embers 138
Scared 145
Middling Management 147
After You......................................165
Unlimited 171
    1: Football 171
    2: Basketball 181
    3: Wrestling 186
    4: Basketball Again 192

Introduction

The stories in this book started with one purpose and ended with another.

I lived in Seattle for most of my adult life and had no reason to think I would live anywhere else. That's when I met Kathy, my wife-to-be, who was born and raised in Michigan. She moved to Seattle, we got married, and I expected that we would stay together in Washington for a long, long time.

It didn't work out that way. For reasons I describe later, we moved from Washington back to Michigan.

Let's just say that the move changed my perspective. Suddenly I was surrounded by new family, new work, and new weather, both literally and metaphorically. Some of it was confusing and upsetting. (Ice storms? In April?? *Come on!*), while other things expanded my imagination.

One of the ways I dealt with it all was to write about it, starting from the moment Kathy and I landed in Michigan. I wrote long letters to the people I left behind in Seattle, telling them about the struggle just to get to Michigan, find a job, and to keep it once I had it. I wrote about how living with my new family felt like a skipping contest near an open mineshaft. And I wrote about living in a state where I could expect to live half of every June in our bathroom during a tornado watch.

The people who got the letters thanked me and said what a strange place I had moved to. "Uh-huh," I said, and kept writing. The first stories in this book, from "Journey to Michigan" to "Halloween Party" all come from those early days.

Then the what-have-I-gotten-myself-into phase passed and the people I worked with in Seattle drifted away and left Kathy and me to ourselves. The letters back home were not needed as much because, little by little, we were making a home right here.

But I did not stop writing. I continued to write even after we were fully settled in, and the audience grew from people I knew to anyone who would listen, and the subjects I wrote about shifted from the new surroundings to anything that interested me at the moment.

What I found was that I kept coming back to the same themes: building a career, both in business and writing, and making a marriage and a life with Kathy.

Both themes left me a lot to work with. Witness the fumbling attempts to be romantic ("Flowers", "My Darling Husband", "Valentine's Day Surprise") and share common interests ("Rush at the DTE", "Blue is a Boy"), and make me presentable to the world ("Captain Pants"), and even live under the same roof together ("Your Big Ass Clogs My Living Room", "After You", "Ladybug Kill, Kill, Kill").

If being married hasn't been easy, neither has trying to achieve wealth, fame, or professional respect. Behold the time I submitted a piece of writing once and was rejected twice ("Rejection...again"), the time I was not hired for a job because I could not put names in alphabetical order ("Job Search"), and the time I locked the keys in my car on the first day I was promoted to a new job ("Middling Management").

Now it is time to widen the circle even further. You have in your hands the written record of one husband and one wife trying to navigate the ups and downs of life. I would have thought, dear reader, you'd have enough struggles of your own without buying a book full of new ones. But hey - it just goes to show you never can tell what people will like.

Anyway, I'll be grateful and not ask too many questions. Thank you so much for your patronage. Please enjoy the stories with our compliments.

Charlie and Kathy Close
Grand Blanc, MI, USA
2008

Acknowledgements

As anyone who has ever spent time with someone writing a book understands, no book is ever written without help from others, be it creatively, editorially, genealogically, hygienically, or therapeutically. I am indebted to many people.

First and foremost, to my wife Kathy, who supported my writing, improved it, and was the frequent subject of it. None of this work would have been possible, or necessary, without her.

To my parents Susan Huntley and Terry Close, who passed on their love of books, culture, humor, and learning going back as far as I can remember. They taught me that to be alive is to be a student.

To the early readers of these stories: Alan Buck, Kathie Brittain Hawken, Corkey Christensen, Larry Coppenrath, John Creason, Yulu Dai, Rachel Howard, Mara Krieps, Jessica Plesko, Maria Raisys, Marissa Simoni, and Kristi Yankacy.

To the early audiences who listened to my readings and podcasts: Garret Gaw, Sonja Gaw, Mary Kupres, Leslie Owens, Lynette Scaffede, Bonnie Standen, Julie Stott, Melanie Sulfaro, and Gene Varnado II.

To the editors of the text of this book: Bonnie Standen and Karen Mulvihill-Younglove. Their criticism showed me flaws I had missed and let me look at the text with fresh eyes.

To the friends and family I found here in Michigan: Marti Konetzka, Frank Konetzka, Tammy Konetzka, Holly Simoni, and all my new nieces and nephews.

And last, but not least, to Kathy again, who is the alpha and omega of my life.

Journey to Michigan

This is the story of the move my wife Kathy and I made across the country from Seattle, Washington to eastern Michigan and the hardships we encountered along the way. But that is not the beginning, not really. To tell about the move, I have to start farther back, when Kathy and I first met.

Kathy grew up in Flint, Michigan. We met through Kathy's Aunt Kim while Kim lived in Seattle.

One day when we were eating lunch Kim said to me, "I've got someone you should meet."

Being a young man looking for love, I said, "Great! Where is she?" I looked around. The lunch room was empty.

"Michigan," said Aunt Kim.

"Michigan?" I said. Michigan, I found out later, was 2,400 miles and three time zones away.

"That's right," said Kim. "You should write to her."

Meanwhile Aunt Kim was working on Kathy, trying hard to get her to answer my letter if I ever wrote one.

I did write to Kathy eventually. In my own mind our first date was on the Saturday night nine years ago when, sitting alone in my apartment, I wrote that first letter.

Letters led to phone calls, and phone bills that exceeded my rent, and phone calls led to visits, and finally, a year after the first letter, Kathy moved out west to live with me.

Kathy had a hard time in Seattle. Even with all the charms of our new life together she still felt a long, long way from home. She did not like living in the middle of a big, loud city.

She felt cramped in the little apartment in the University District with its banging steam pipes, its bathroom without a shower curtain, and the gas stove whose pilot light had not been lit since the 1970s. The city's natural beauty and its energetic cultural scene did not make up for the loss of family and familiar surroundings.

While Kathy struggled to turn my bachelor home and bachelor life into a homey place for the two of us together, my career as a software consultant began to climb upward. Seattle was a great place for software in the late 1990s. Microsoft was just down the road and it was a hotbed for startup technology companies second only to Silicon Valley. During those years I worked on projects for several companies, large and small, spanning four continents, and I learned the basics of my profession.

The uninterrupted rise continued until I got a job as a consultant for a dot-com whose product saved millions of dollars for Fortune 500 companies. Because I was working for a good company with a good product and good customers, and because the company was a dot-com startup, and because it was the late 1990s, I had the completely reasonable expectation of making millions dollars in a hurry and retiring before I turned forty. I was, after all, reinventing the nature of business for the twenty-first century. If it didn't take the whole century to do it, why not cash out my stock options early and buy a yacht?

Then reality took over. The clouds stopped raining gold coins, and the rivers stopped flowing hot chocolate, and gravity began to pull down, not up, once again.

In reality, my company, like many other startups, was a young company in a fledgling market, swimming upstream and trying to sell to much larger, stronger, and slower companies. It was prone to rookie mistakes and it was vulnerable to the economic downturn that started in 2000. Rather than spreading millions to its employees, it began to lay them off by the sackful, until finally the company was bought out by its chief competitor and most of my coworkers were laid off.

And, in reality, I was a competent business consultant and software engineer with excellent experience and prospects, on the cusp of joining junior management. In other words, there was no way I would have ever made millions unless the executives were about to make billions. Which they weren't.

Now that I might not become a millionaire after all, it was time to rethink what I wanted to do. Kathy had something to say about that. She wanted to return home, and I, no longer held aloft by the dream of creating the future of business technology and reaping the rewards, agreed.

We started boxing up our apartment in early March. Books on bookshelves turned into boxes, forgotten software hiding in drawers turned into boxes, CDs turned into boxes, porcelain decorations turned into boxes, pictures hanging on walls turned into boxes, computer equipment turned into boxes, a kitchen full of dishes turned into boxes, closets full of stuff we never looked at turned into boxes, and by the time we were through, all we owned was boxes.

It seemed fitting and proper that we should return our belongings to boxes, since most of them had started out in a box, having been delivered by UPS or brought home from the store. Think of it as the circle of life: ashes to ashes, box to box.

And so our life was surrounded by boxes and our home was filled with the incense of cardboard. In March we left them behind for a few weeks to drive to Michigan to find a place to live, and when we got back they were still there, self-contained. They looked happy to see us, but not like they missed us very much.

I should clarify something here about our packing. We weren't *totally* packed. It wasn't *all* done. The thing about packing was that the more of it we did, the more there was to do. There was always one more closet to empty and things that couldn't be packed until the last day, so that the state of being done was a mirage we could always see but never reach. We spent several weeks like this, picking away at things. We prepared a little more each day, but mostly we waited.

More than once Kathy said to me, "I want to go *now*," and I would say we can't. It wasn't the plan we had worked out, and it was 8:00 at night, and there was a basketball game on the TV: we weren't going anywhere.

Finally, when Kathy's brother Butch arrived from Flint, it was time, at last, to start moving. His job was to add muscle - not a problem at 6'3" and looking like a bald, red-goateed pro wrestler. He also brought experience. He was a diesel mechanic and was used to working with heavy equipment, so driving the moving truck would not be a problem for him. Kathy and I had never driven anything bigger than a station wagon.

Butch was about to spend his first night in Seattle and Kathy and I were about to spend our last. We ordered dinner from the local Thai restaurant and ate it cross-legged on the floor, and then rolled over and went to sleep. Tomorrow was going to be a long day.

We rose early the next morning, drank a pot of coffee, and got to work. Butch and I went to get the U-Haul and the car dolly. We planned to load the truck with the contents of our home, pull the car behind, and have the three of us ride in the front seat of the truck.

Pursuant to that plan, we started hauling boxes and furniture down the apartment building steps and up the ramp of the U-Haul. The single hardest part of the day came first, with the moving of our desk. The desk was the heaviest thing we owned and it felt like it was made of cast iron encased in lead. We heaved it into the U-Haul, and once we set the desk down I told Butch that the worst was over and the day was practically done. Ha-ha, old buddy, high-five!

He didn't say anything, which made him wiser than I.

We hauled box after box while Kathy stayed in the apartment and helped see that things got emptied in proper order. Butch stayed in the truck and loaded it up so tight that no light could get through the cracks. I worked in between and ferried piles of boxes on a hand truck, and made myself popular with the neighbors next to the stairwell by rolling the hand truck down one banging step at a time.

Optimism reigned supreme for the first few hours. We were still strong and the truck looked as empty as the inside of an old man's mouth. Then doubt began to find purchase in our sweat and tiring muscles. The question was this: which was greater, the unfillable truck or the unemptiable apartment? At first the truck seemed to be winning, but as the rooms of the apartment barely began to be emptied, and as Butch filled the truck past the wheel wells, we started to lose confidence.

Kathy was the first to see it. She subtracted the space required from the space remaining and came up with red ink. Kathy said, "It's not all going to fit." Butch, a graduate of the school of you-can't-stop-me-unless-you-kill-me, said, "Yeah it will. I'll make it fit." I didn't know the answer, but wanted to be strong for Kathy, so I said, "Hang in there. We're going to be fine."

Eventually we all saw that Kathy was right: the apartment would win. The unloaded things took up too much room and each item felt like a blow to the sternum.

...the cushions on the couch - *BAM*

...all the Christmas decorations in the storage closet - *POW*

...the guitar amplifier and the file cabinet in the office - *WHACK*.

So what to do now? We couldn't get a bigger truck on such short notice, and even if we could we didn't want to have to unload the old truck into the new truck. Our mime fists went to our eyes in silent sobbing at the thought.

Butch got us unstuck. He said to call U-Haul to reserve a trailer that we could tow behind the truck. Kathy made the call, got the trailer, and so we were saved. Surely we couldn't fill a truck *and* a trailer. However, it also meant that we wouldn't be able to tow the car. We would have to drive it along with the truck.

Now that we had a both a truck and a trailer we were able to conquer the bottomless apartment - barely. We filled the trailer first, and when it was very, very full I watched Butch pull the door down. He pulled, yanked, and sunk his teeth into the door strap for extra leverage.

I looked away. Some things are necessary but should never be witnessed. It was enough to know that Butch won the fight with the trailer door.

The truck door came next, and again Butch was the winner. His head is made for squishing things into a U-Haul. It's bald and very hard on the inside with a thick soft covering on the outside. He pulled the door down, and when it was a foot away from the latch he jammed his head against the mattress that held the rest of the contents still. He pushed until he could shut the door, just *this* close to decapitating himself.

The truck and trailer were loaded with no room to spare - a nice day's work. The problem was, the day's work was not done. In order to stay on schedule we still had to get to Spokane, where my father and my step mom Barbara had offered to put us up for the night. It was Thursday and Butch had to return to work the following Tuesday. It was already well into the evening by the time we finished loading, and we wouldn't get to Spokane before midnight even if we drove fast.

Kathy and Butch got in the U-Haul and I drove the car. One blessing of having to drive two vehicles was that we didn't have to fit all three of us into the cab of the truck. It was a big truck but we were three big people. The "middle" seat was barely a seat at all, and Kathy, the baby of our group, would have had to sit in it for 2,400 miles.

We had wanted to tow the car instead of driving it separately. Driving the car would put mileage on it, make it necessary to communicate and coordinate between the two vehicles, and it would mean that someone would always be driving alone. But the truck was too small, so we had to do it anyway.

It turned out that was one of the luckiest breaks of the whole trip.

The truck was a rolling adventure, a little Six Flags in an orange and white box with wheels. On the one hand it lacked power. Going up the Cascade Mountains it had to pull and strain like The Little U-Haul That Could to make it up to the summit.

Keeping the momentum in the U-Haul was extremely important, because if it wasn't kept, the truck would have rolled to a stop, then rolled back down I-90 the way it came, picking up speed with Butch steering by the rearview mirror, and it would not have stopped until it flew backwards off a pier into Puget Sound.

Halfway up the mountains Butch and Kathy had to pass me because I was not going fast enough for them. Kathy waved to me as I passed, and I thought she was taunting me: "Keep up, slowpoke!" I thought it was cute and waved back. I didn't find out until later that she was waving in panic: "Get me out of here, Charlie!" Kathy, it turned out, didn't like to ride in wobbly trucks at 90 mph.

On the other hand, the truck also lacked good brakes. Butch and Kathy had not noticed while climbing that the brakes were not built to handle such a heavy load. While descending the mountains, however, this weakness stood out like a bowling ball on a water slide. I was fortunate, driving in front, that I didn't have to watch as they took the turns in the road at rollercoaster high speed. If the truck rocked and heaved airborne a few times, I didn't notice. It was dark outside and I was paying attention to the road in front of me. Safety first.

The truck also lacked a modern suspension system. There were no shock absorbers, no springs, nothing to keep from feeling every ridge and dent on the highway. I had once ridden in a truck down a "road" that was actually a dry creek bed full of rounded boulders. That was a very bouncy ride, so I could empathize with Butch and Kathy.

The truck would turn out to have additional drawbacks, but more on that later.

We made our first stop after the mountains in Vantage to get gas. I got out of the car and walked over to Kathy while Butch went into the station to find the restroom. She looked like she was about to cry. "How are you doing?" I asked.

"I've been missing you *so* much! If we're going to die I want us to be together." She told me about almost crashing into me from behind while climbing the mountains.

"Don't worry," I said. "We'll be fine." And we were fine, but saying so didn't take the slapped look off her face.

An interesting thing happened to us at Vantage. I tried to pay for gas with my credit card and was declined, which had never happened before. I told Kathy and she got on her cell phone to the credit card company while I went in to pay cash for the gas and get some dinner out of a cold case.

Kathy found out that the card was declined because there was $11,000 of outstanding authorizations from U-Haul on it, taking the card past its credit limit. That didn't make sense to us, since the U-Haul had cost only $2,600. Kathy put it together when she remembered that the agent behind the U-Haul counter had been having trouble with his computer and had swiped the card several times in order to create one charge. Think of them as practice swings before stepping up to the plate. To the card company, however, each swipe was serious and legally binding. So…very sorry, but no more credit. The card company advised us to call U-Haul to get them to call to explain that most of the swipes were do-overs.

We reached Spokane at about 12:30 in the morning and fell into bed without taking showers. We got up slowly the next morning and had breakfast with Dad and Barbara. Kathy asked Butch if he would be offended if she rode with me.

"I can't get in that truck again," she said.

Butch said he wouldn't be offended, and Kathy said, "Thank you!" From there on Kathy joined me in the car while Butch drove solo. That was our lucky break. In the end only Butch had to drive in the truck, and for that we were thankful.

After breakfast we said goodbye to Dad and Barbara, and headed east.

Our plan was to take I-90 from Spokane to Billings, Montana where we would switch onto I-94. We wanted to get as far as we could, but weren't sure how far we could go in one day.

Butch was ready to go hard. "Let's just drive it straight through."

Kathy and I weren't as sure. When we had made this drive in March we had only gotten as far as Billings, and we knew that the next big town was Bismarck. We didn't want to end up in the middle of North Dakota with nowhere to sleep for two hundred miles.

The challenge of crossing Idaho and Montana was the same challenge as crossing the Cascades - only more. The Rocky Mountains form a wall across the Western states. Up 7,000 feet and down 3,000 feet at steep grade along a curvy highway. By this time, Kathy and I were driving behind Butch instead of in front. It seemed better to let the slower vehicle set the pace. When driving uphill the truck pulled the wobbly trailer, but when rolling downhill the trailer pushed the truck.

Any bump made them both bounce and twist in opposite directions like a dog shaking off water.

We stopped at a rest area for lunch. Butch stumbled out of the U-Haul looking like he had ridden three hours inside a rattling grain silo, which was pretty much true except for the grain. Kathy made sandwiches using the lid of a can of Vienna sausages to spread the peanut butter and jelly, and Butch told stories about the times he had almost run off the road or crushed another car. Kathy and I chewed our sandwiches, quiet and wide-eyed.

Despite the truck nearly rocking and swaying off the road with all our possessions, we enjoyed the beauty of western Montana. The highway passed alongside Missoula on an adjacent ridge. From there it looked like a city built from a model kit, with tiny, perfect houses and streets. You could see all of it at once, nestled up against a flinty wall of mountains. The view was huge and intimate at the same time. The city seemed to fit tongue-in-groove with the mountains, and fragile enough to disappear completely if they should collapse.

The journey from the Montana state line to Billings was like that the whole way. Olive rolling hills and swaths of grass reached out to the distant mountains tipped with snow. We passed through in the late afternoon, when the sun was starting to sink and it and cast hard shadows on the lee side of the hills. Bright here, black there. Hazy here, eye-wateringly clear there. We drove through a chiaroscuro of not only light, but also of space. We could see every detail as if it were a few feet away even though most of the surroundings were miles distant - sharp contrasts of near and far and big and small condensed into the same scale.

We decided to spend the night in Billings. We could have gone further, we all agreed, but we had worked very hard the day before and were running low on sleep. Better to pull over for the night, get a good rest, and put in a long day tomorrow.

Billings is 550 miles from Spokane, and I thought we had met our goal by getting this far on the first day. We still weren't sure how long it was going to take us to get all the way home. At this rate it would take four days, and we wouldn't find out until tomorrow how hard we were willing to push.

Butch said, "Let's go for it."

Kathy said, "Let's get there in one piece."

During the day Kathy had called U-Haul to explain the situation with the credit card. The U-Haul person said he would look into it. Kathy called the card company when we reached the motel in Billings and found out that not only were the extra authorizations dropped but so was the correct $2,600 charge. "Good news!" we thought, but cautiously. We were glad to have our card back in service, but if the correct U-Haul charges were missing, some more "activity" was going to happen on the card, and we didn't know whether it would be usable afterward. But it was usable now, and that was good enough. We put the motel charge on the card as if it were brand new.

We ate dinner at the Cracker Barrel, our favorite Billings restaurant. The Cracker Barrel specializes in serving good food to America's travelers: hamburgers, pot roast, chicken, and the like. Nothing fancy, just good food for good people.

When Kathy and I stopped in Billings in March we weren't sure what route we were going to take to Michigan. The road forked at Billings. I-90 continued on through South Dakota, and I-94 ran through North Dakota. The roads met up again in Madison, Wisconsin. We didn't know which way would be better and we were going to flip a coin, but instead we asked the waitress at the Cracker Barrel, who told us to take I-94. We did, and it was good advice.

The next morning at 6:00 AM we ate breakfast again at our favorite Billings restaurant, the Cracker Barrel, where they served six varieties of biscuits and gravy, four varieties of pancakes and French toast, and three types of fruit cup for breakfast, along with all the coffee we could drink.

Butch asked the waitress what kinds of omelets they had.

She told him that they served Cheese, Ham & Cheese, Bacon & Cheese, Sausage & Cheese, and Western.

Butch asked her if the Western omelet came with cheese.

"Yes it does," she said.

Butch said he'd have the Western and the waitress asked him what he'd like for his side dish - hash browns, toast, or hash brown casserole. Butch asked if the casserole was good. She said it was, and he said he'd take it. And it was good, too. When the waitress set it on the table in front of Butch we found out that hash brown casserole is hash browns with melted cheese.

It was a good day for driving. The land smoothed out from hilly to flat after Billings. No more mountains for Butch, thank God. The scenery was more sparse and less dramatic, mostly farms and grassland in all directions.

All the towns were small. None contained more than a few hundred people, and they looked not like towns as much as camping sites with buildings instead of tents. Kathy and I wondered what people did for work out here. Did Amazon.com deliver here? Where did the kids come from to fill the school? Was there a school at all? Where were the other schools to play football against?

We had purchased a AAA membership before we left so that we would have roadside assistance. Out in eastern Montana roadside assistance felt like a laughably foolish thing to expect. Assistance from *where?* Cell phone signal to call AAA from *where?* We could forget about AAA.

You had to buy gas when you could in that part of the country, not when you wanted to, since the next pump might be a hundred miles away. Same for lodging, food, and anything else. Butch didn't understand at first how far apart everything was. I would ask him how the truck was doing for gas and he'd say, "Great - over a quarter tank." To me that was trouble waiting to happen and I made sure we pulled over at the next exit.

Our goal was to drive far enough that we could drive the rest of the way home the next day. Par would be Fargo, North Dakota, where we had spent the second night during the March trip. Fargo was just west of the Minnesota border and a bit too far from home to reach it in one day. We wanted to get farther if possible. Early in the morning we were ambitious and thought we could make it to Milwaukee - that is, through the rest of Montana and all of North Dakota, Minnesota, and Wisconsin. Milwaukee lay an hour north of Chicago and about eight hours from our new home.

By lunchtime we did not feel as ambitious, for two reasons. First, the next big town after Billings was Bismarck, North Dakota, and Bismarck was half way across the state. Call it human psychology, but when we left Billings we felt like we were just a short hop to the North Dakota border, but it took hours of driving just to get through Montana, longer to get to Bismarck, and Bismarck was only a milestone, not a real destination. By the time we reached it, some of our *joie de vivre* had dissipated.

Second, time and tedium aside, the drive to Bismarck was harder work than expected. Something to understand about eastern Montana and all of North Dakota: the land there was as flat and wide open as a Cracker Barrel pancake. With nothing to interrupt it, the wind has its way. It blew all day long across eastern Montana and North Dakota - hard, cold, and gusty.

Meanwhile, the only thing flatter and wider than the North Dakota prairie is the side of a 17-foot U-Haul. Not only did the truck drive like a rolling cement mixer, it handled like three sails to the wind. Most of I-94 was two lanes in each direction, one to drive on and one to get blown into. Butch needed four hands to drive it, two for gripping the wheel and two for praying. Kathy and I watched from behind as the truck weaved and twisted. She was torn between closing her eyes so she wouldn't have to watch Butch crash, and keeping them open to give him strength.

Butch didn't make it any easier for Kathy. He believed the truck handled the wind better at 80 mph than 60 mph: "It's a lot better," he said. "Seriously." Whether we lived or died we were going to get there fast.

We stopped for gas in Bismarck. Butch got out of the truck, teetered over to me, and looked at me with eyes that had seen the inside of a tornado. "Whooooooo!" he hollered. "That truck is some fun! YEAH!"

Kathy hurried over to Butch, arms outstretched. "Oh, honey, are you all right? Come here…"

"Oh, yeah," he answered. "No problem." Of course someone could take a shovel to back of his head and he'd say "No problem." To Butch, no problem is code for, "It's a son of a bitch but it hasn't killed me yet."

We kept going, and Butch hung in there. We continued through Fargo, still not sure how far we could get. After we reached Minnesota we decided we should spend the night somewhere west of Minneapolis. We could have kept going into Wisconsin but if we had we wouldn't have been able to get an early start the next day.

The town we settled on was St. Cloud, about an hour outside the Twin Cities. It was nighttime and we were tired and ready to get some sleep.

We stopped for gas before looking for a motel. Surprise! Our card was declined again, and so was the alternate card. Kathy called customer service for each one. The alternate card had been shut off because charges were being made far from home. It looked like someone had stolen the card and started running east. Kathy explained that we were moving, and the card was reactivated. The main card, however, the one with the U-Haul charges, was more difficult. Kathy had to explain to the representative that she had given all our information to another rep in Billings, so they should have it on file already. She had to explain it four times before the rep would put the card back in service. "I'm in a gas station in St. Cloud, Minnesota and I can't get gas!" said Kathy. "I already explained all that to so-and-so yesterday and to someone-or-other the night before. This makes three days in a row I've had to call you guys!"

Getting a motel room was also more difficult than expected. There was a Holiday Inn right next to the gas station, but I didn't want to go there because they had been nasty about letting us stay with our dog in March, so we drove halfway across the city to the next nearest motel. No luck there: full up. Then we drove around to another motel: full up there too. By this time Kathy was so tired she could barely stand and just wanted to get into a damn bed. It was not fun to walk out of the second place and tell Kathy we would have to keep looking. No it wasn't. I put pride aside and we went back to the Holiday Inn.

Full there too! It turned out that six local religious colleges were holding commencement the next day and the whole town was full of proud moms and dads. If someone had wanted to meet all the Lutheran parents over the age of fifty, the place to go was St. Cloud that night.

That's when we caught a break. The man at the desk at the Holiday Inn made a phone call to the motel across the street and got us a room. Thank you, Holiday Inn. I forgive you for dissing our dog.

We intended to push from St. Cloud all the way home, no matter how long it took. We thought we had seen the worst after driving through the wind of the high plains. One more day of solid driving, not even that hard, and we would be home.

Not so. The wind in Minnesota and Wisconsin was even worse than North Dakota. Tornadoes and heavy storm fronts were passing to the south. We caught the edge of these storms, and I can say from personal experience that driving through sub-hurricane strength rain and wind was very, very difficult.

Butch believed the truck handled better going fast than slow even in hurricanes. He drove straight into the weather and Kathy and I did our best to keep up. If you've ever driven through a car wash you know how cozy it is to hear the wash of water and not be able to see out the windows. It's very soothing, isn't it? Now try it at 80 mph while chasing after a blurry orange truck.

We hit Minneapolis first thing in the morning and we had no problem getting through. We whizzed past the city of glassy skyscrapers and ornate German churches and sighed with relief when we passed into Wisconsin. The day's travels included driving through three big cities: Minneapolis, Milwaukee, and Chicago. One down, two to go.

The grind began in earnest after Minneapolis. The wind whipped up strong and the rain came down hard. We got our biggest scare driving through Milwaukee. I-94 passes through the center of town on a raised bridge from which you can see in all directions: all the old churches, breweries, and the baseball stadium. I had enjoyed it when we drove through in March and looked forward to stealing a few glances around from behind the steering wheel.

However, just as we rounded onto the bridge a gust of wind struck the car across the side and pushed us two lanes over. I skidded back into control of the car and Butch swiveled back and forth in the U-Haul like it had been slapped, and that was the end of the sight-seeing.

Okay, I was humble now. Just drive, Charlie. Just drive. Butch had experienced most of the wind problems up to that point. The car I was driving didn't put as much sail into the wind. For the rest of the trip, however, I had to wrestle the wind too. Mostly I could drive without difficulty until, without warning, I was ten feet to the left and trying to stay in the saddle. Think of it like plugging in an old blow dryer in a bathtub full of water. It's just like plugging it in an empty tub - until it isn't.

And so it went, past Milwaukee and into Chicago. Like Milwaukee I had been hoping to take in some of the scenery, and like Milwaukee the weather made it impossible. Chicago, being Chicago, was ready to give us an old fashioned ass whipping. Driving through the city was as cold and grim as playing against the Bears. Later I heard news reports that the wind gusts there had reached over 100 mph.

And more of the same past Chicago, through Indiana and up through southern and western Michigan. Driving through an upper Midwest storm is all about holding on and pushing forward. Three hundred miles to go, then two-sixty, then two-twenty, then one-eighty…

And, at about 8:30 that night, we arrived at Kathy's sister's house. Kathy pulled me out of the car with my hands stuck in a claw position. I asked, "Where's the bed? Where's the bed?" I was ready to sleep for a hundred hours.

But not Kathy. There were things to do, as there always were at the end of a trip, no matter how long or how tiring. Unload the car first and get a load of laundry started? Um, okay, no problem. Where is that bed again?

Our hard driving had paid off. We reached our destination in only three days, landing there on Mother's Day. It didn't matter so much to Kathy or me, but Butch was able to drive the U-Haul back to his house and hug his wife and kids hard.

We met Butch at our new place the next morning to unload. As he had promised, the truck and trailer unloaded much faster than they had loaded, and we had extra help from Butch's young daughters. The boxes we had last seen in Seattle had suddenly reappeared in our new place. Ah, back to boxes!

The next day we started taking everything out of boxes and putting the contents where they belonged. Kathy and her sister Marti did the bulk of the work, and I carried empty boxes and items that we didn't need back to our storage unit.

There isn't much to say about the apartment. In a way, after so much work, having our home back and all put together feels a bit like an anticlimax, except that it feels *good.* Kathy's things look as good as ever. My new office feels much more spacious than the old one. Life is almost back to normal now after weeks of waiting, and working, and waiting some more. Once we both have jobs the transition will be complete. Fingers crossed.

We were looking for a change: I wanted a different hill to climb and Kathy just wanted to come back home. Now here we are.

Life is good.

Job Search

My job search has been progressing smoothly and has given me every satisfaction I could wish for, except a job.

I had forgotten how depressing it is. I haven't had to look for a job for eight years, the summer the contract expired on a job that I had held for nearly five years. It was also when Kathy, my wife-to-be, came to live with me.

"Seattle is cool!" she told me one day soon after she arrived. She had found a job at a veterinary hospital in less than two weeks.

I, on the other hand, had been out of work for a month. "The regional technology job market is going through a soft phase," I told her. At least it was for me.

Then Windows 95 was released with the biggest, most publicized technology launch in my working life, and three weeks later I started a new job at Microsoft.

Since then I have advanced steadily in business software consulting: upward and onward. That is, until I quit to move to Michigan.

I had considered staying with my current employer in some kind of loose leave-of-absence arrangement, but in the end I decided to resign. It was better to make a clean break. A cross-country move is a little bit like being a fireman. Similar to a fireman, my day was taken up with unpredictable fits of preparation, hard work, waiting, and occasional panic. Working on software, however, takes long stretches of unbroken calm and contemplation that are not easily found in the rumble seat of a fire truck. Even after we arrived in Michigan there were days of things to do to get fully entrenched in our new home. Services had to be connected. Supplies had to be purchased. Cars had to be maintained. The list went on and on. The calendar, far from furling cleanly out before me, looked more like the Stars and Stripes at Fort McHenry.

Not that I didn't try to land a job even from the beginning. I posted my résumé on several job websites after I resigned, which created the first challenge, that of communicating plans and expectations to potential employers. I had several conversations with recruiters that went something like this.

I said, "I'm ready to interview immediately, at least over the phone, but I can't work until I'm settled in Michigan."

"When will you be settled?"

"I don't know exactly. Probably some time in May. And we'll be in Michigan in March to find a place to live."

"So you're going to be here in March?"

"Right, for a few weeks."

"You're not moving here?"

"Yes I am, but in two stages. First find a place to live. Then come back and move all our belongings. I'll be out for the first stage soon."

"You could interview then?"

"Sure."

"But you're in...Seattle...now?" I could hear the recruiter look down to read the address on my résumé.

"Right - for a few more days."

"And you're coming here when?"

"I'm leaving in about a week. My wife and I are driving it."

"Really! How long does that take?"

"Well, I don't know yet. Between three days and a week, we think."

"Wow. And then you could be available for an interview?"

"Sure."

"And that puts us out to...looks like...early April. Sound about right?"

"I think so."

"Well good. I'll keep your name on file and we'll see if we can get something lined up for you when you get here. Sound good?"

"Sure."

"Okay then."

All these conversations with recruiters were followed by a silent telephone. None of them called back, and I was not surprised. I did not make much progress on the job hunt before the move, due in part, I'm sure, to living neither here nor there. Despite trying to explain what I was looking for, and where, and when, I think I created more confusion than understanding.

I had a couple of particularly interesting conversations during that phase. One was from a company I'll call Rooster Technologies. Rooster Technologies is a consulting and outplacement firm to whom I had sent my résumé.

I think the recruiter at Rooster Technologies was impressed with my résumé because she acted on it first thing in the morning, at 8:30 AM Detroit time, or 5:30 Seattle time, when I was still sleeping.

If I had known she was going to call I would have made preparations - like wearing clothes. But never mind, I was ready. We spoke for a few minutes about my experience, interests, and background, and she asked me to take an online technical skills test. In particular the test was supposed to measure my knowledge of J2EE.

For the benefit of people who may not know this, J2EE stands for "Java 2 Enterprise Edition." It is a collection of related technologies that let developers create software for common tasks, like building web sites, querying data from databases, and sending and receiving email.

There are dozens of specific J2EE technologies and they are complex enough that almost any software developer knows some of them better than others. This is the case for me as well. I could teach classes in some of the technologies, and I am only a student in others.

For that reason, any test on J2EE is a gamble. Would I be tested on what I knew, or what I didn't?

I mostly lost the gamble with the test given to me by Rooster Technologies. It emphasized topics that I did not know well, although I knew enough to make educated guesses.

After taking the test the recruiter called me back. "Good news," she said. "You scored in the 89th percentile."

"Great," I said.

And with a few more words we hung up, and I have not heard from her since.

What saddens me isn't that I was able to score in the 89th percentile largely on the strength of my ability to guess. No, what saddens me is that all the knowledge I have earned fair and square squeezes neatly in that last eleven percent.

The other interesting conversation was actually two conversations with a company I'll call Chicken George Partners. Chicken George is a consulting and outplacement firm.

The first call was from a woman named Melissa. She asked me a few questions about my experience, interests, and background, and she told me about an opening she had for a software architect at a startup company in Bellevue, Washington.

"No, no," I told her. "I'm actually looking for work in the Detroit area. I think I put that at the top of my résumé."

"Oh," she answered. She didn't want to say so, but the influence of Chicken George Partners did not reach all the way to Detroit. Perhaps, I thought, it got about as far as Bozeman, Montana and then trailed off.

I said I was sorry if it was not clear I was not looking for work in Washington State. She said sorry for the confusion and good luck on your future search. I said thanks and that was the last I expected to hear from Chicken George.

But it wasn't. That afternoon I got a call from Benjamin. He was from Chicken George too, and wanted to tell me about an opportunity in Redmond, Washington.

I listened until he finished, and said, "Actually, I spoke with Melissa this morning. You talk to her at all?"

"You bet I know Melissa. But listen, she and I are working on different job orders..."

"Sorry about the mix-up, Benjamin," I said. "She and I were talking about one of *her* job orders this morning and I told her I'm moving to the Detroit area and looking for work there.

"Oh, okay," Benjamin said, and again I imagined the map of the United States in his head with no pins in it near Detroit. "Well good luck to you, and you take care."

"Thanks, Benjamin," I said.

Then Kathy and I drove to Michigan to find a place to live. We stayed with Kathy's sister Marti. I updated my online résumés with her phone number while keeping the Seattle address. No doubt it was confusing for everyone, but in my defense I'll say that I updated as much as I knew as soon as I knew it. If it confused the recruiters, it confused Kathy and me even more.

One potential employer, however, was not confused! Not long after arriving in Michigan I got an email, which said something to this effect.

Dear Mr. Close -

I came across your résumé on [popular job website] and I would like to discuss an opportunity with you in the Farmington Hills area at your earliest convenience. [Company Name] is a major player in the financial services industry. I can be reached at [contact information].

Regards
Elizabeth [Surname]

I did a little checking up on [Company Name], and sure enough it was a big and well-known financial services company, actually a subsidiary of a really, really big and well-known financial services company. And they were in Michigan! And they had found me! I felt like I had finally arrived at my new home. I could see clearly now. The rain was gone.

I was so happy that I actually printed off the email and stood over Kathy while she read it. I bit my lip and held my hands at my sides, wondering if she understood its significance.

"Neat!" said Kathy.

"It's in Farmington Hills!" I said. "Somebody in Michigan found my résumé."

And then she understood and we were both happy together. She was like Dorothy from *The Wizard of Oz*, and I was like the high-stepping munchkin who hooks her by the elbow and dances her around in a circle. Ha ha ha! Ho ho ho!

I called Elizabeth the next day after studying her company's website. I wanted to be prepared.

I said, "Hello. This is Charlie Close. You sent me an email yesterday?"

"Why, hello, Mr. Close. Thanks for calling me back. You've had a chance to look at our website?"

"Yes, ma'am," I said. My preparation had paid off already.

"Good. Then you know that we're a financial services company that specializes in providing investment and financial planning advice to families and individuals."

"Yes, I do." I said. That was clearly on their website.

"Is that a mission you could get excited about, Mr. Close?"

"Certainly," I said. Financial planning is good.

"Good. Then what I'd like to do is schedule you to come to a meeting with some of our senior directors and managers. They'll get a chance to meet you and explain everything in greater detail. If all goes well, I can set up an interview. Sound good?"

Now I was confused. Why was there a meeting before an interview, and why would a bunch of senior managers and directors want to talk to a newbie like me, and why did I have the feeling I would not be the only candidate invited to this meeting?

"Excuse me," I said. "Just wondering - what exactly is the job?"

Elizabeth said, "Of course. The job is providing investment and financial planning advice to families and individuals."

"Oh," I said.

"We've found that people with your background usually do very well. Do you believe in keeping your options open?"

"Sure I do," I said.

"Then I think this opportunity would be a good one for you. You see - "

"I'm sorry. I've been doing information technology for ten years now and I think that's the kind of work I'm looking for."

"As I said, people of your background have been especially successful here in the past. We could - "

"I'm sorry. I'm just not interested, but thanks for your time."

And that was the end of that. I had to walk out of the bedroom where I had gone for privacy and let Kathy know that the opportunity had not worked out. Ha ha ha. Ho ho ho.

It was at about the same time that I received a call from a hoarse-sounding woman with a Brooklyn accent named Nina.

"Mr. Close?"

"Yes," I said.

"Good evening, sir. How are you today?"

"I'm good. Thanks."

"That's good. The reason I'm calling is that I understand you recently left your employment. Is that correct, sir?"

"Yes..." I said.

"Well I know that can be a very stressful experience. The reason I'm calling is that I provide financial counseling to people in your situation. There is a lot you can do to get the most out of your COBRA health insurance and your 401(k) that most people don't know about. Do you think that would be helpful to someone like yourself?"

The conversation did not go much farther. I cut it short and wondered how people like Nina could find me so quickly but not people who could offer me a real job.

Even though these calls did not turn in to a job, I choose to accentuate the positive and eliminate the negative. My very presence, though unemployed, was helping to keep the wheels of industry turning. I served a purpose, and that is what is so great about our economy: nothing in it is wasted.

I kept looking, chin up and chest out, and soon I reached the interview stage for another job, this one better suited to my skills. It was for a startup software company in Livonia that makes business software for large organizations to help them reduce cost and improve legal compliance, which closely resembled the kind of product I worked on for the last five years. So far, so good.

I applied for the job and received a request to do a phone screen interview. Excellent, I thought. I assumed the call would be from a member of the company's human resources department wanting to ask general questions about my experience, interests, and background.

But it wasn't. The call was from the wife of the company's chief technology officer and she came packing bigger hardware. For most of an hour she asked me detailed technical questions designed to discover how familiar I was with the technology they used to build their product. It went very well. She stayed almost completely inside my eleven percent and I handled the questions easily, and the questions, while not the most difficult imaginable, were tough enough to show I wasn't bluffing. Near the end I started whistling "Sweet Georgia Brown" in my head. Was it a definitive technical test? No, but I had passed, and it was good enough to get me a face-to-face interview.

Shot. Buzzer. *Swish.*

I arrived at the interview in jacket and tie and I immediately got a sense of the good old days back at my last job. I was hired there as one of the first seventy-five employees, a small company even by startup standards. It was still possible for everyone to know everyone.

It looked much the same here at first glance. It was housed in an office building located in a semi-industrial suburb of Detroit where the rent is reasonable. The company fit inside one large room full of cubicles. I didn't know what the dress code would be, but I needn't have worried. Corporate casual was the upper end. Mostly there were jeans, shorts, and T-shirts, and no one I saw was over the age of forty.

The interview was with a fellow I'll call Meadowlark. He was one of two lead engineers on a ten-person development team. I tried to prepare by looking him up on the Internet and came away impressed. This guy had his own side business making software tools, and also contributed to other software projects. I expected him to ask me some difficult questions.

We talked for the better part of two hours. He talked about the company, the kind of work it did, and what he thought it needed to improve. He described the kind of work that might be expected of me, and the more I listened the more it sounded like my prior experience. I chimed in from time to time with observations about things my old company had done well and mistakes it had made. Ah, I thought, so much possibility and so much work to do.

During this time he asked only one or two technical questions. The most difficult was this one, which I have simplified only a little.

"Suppose," Meadowlark said, "you have a computer file with a list of names and you want to use Java to read the list, sort it alphabetically, and output it to the screen. How would you do it?"

I said, "Java provides a class to read files. I don't know its name but I know where to look and I could find it in less than five minutes. Then Java provides the boinkity-boink for storing collections of things. I could read the file into a boinkity-boink and use the built-in boinkity-boink-sorter to sort the boinkity-boink and I could send its contents to the screen."

It was a good answer, I thought. I answered the question completely, and was open about what I didn't know while simultaneously showing that not knowing it was a minor and correctable gap.

"Okay," said Meadowlark. "How would you do it if you did not have the boinkity-boink sorter?"

But I *do* have it, I thought. That's why it was included in Java, so that people like Meadowlark and me would not need to build it ourselves. "Okay. Well I haven't had to write code to sort things since college, but it would not take long to look up a good sorting routine and apply it to the names in the boinkity-boink. There must be a hundred sorting routines out there."

"Okay," said Meadowlark. "But what if you did not have a boinkity-boink at all?"

Not have a boinkity-boink? But that's one of the most basic things in all of Java. When would you ever not have that? Why don't you just drop me naked in a field and tell me to forage for worms and berries?

"A boinkity-boink," I answered, "is just a fancy control panel for a set of pigeonholes that store things. I could work directly with the pigeon holes." ...And I would probably build standard functionality for manipulating the pigeonholes, and in the end I would have built my own boinkity-boink. If you stick around you can watch me build a shelter with chicken bones for nails and a flat rock for a hammer.

"Okay," he said, and that was the end of that question.

And that, literally, was the hardest technical question he asked. Did I answer well? Judge for yourself, but I am satisfied.

The interview ended and he said he would meet with his fellow technical lead and decide what to do next. I shook his hand on the way out, and I could feel that something was off. You can usually tell when you've impressed someone. I did not get that sense here.

A couple of days later Meadowlark sent me an email saying that my technical skills did not meet their needs. I sighed a big sigh. I had gotten a second interview on the strength of my technical skills and lost a third interview on the basis of questions that Meadowlark must have been thinking but didn't ask.

Shot. Buzzer. *Clang!*

Oh well. I wrote down a list of all the things I don't like about small software companies, Livonia, and working without boinkity-boink, and I put it through a paper shredder. Case closed.

It was actually a good experience. I figured if I could get an interview I would have a fair chance to show my best, and if I got enough chances I would find someone to hire me.

Most of the phone calls, however, were from recruiters at consulting and outplacement firms. Many of these companies acted like your date to the junior prom: they wanted to get to second base without getting to know you. I've had a number of conversations that have gone, in whole or in part, like this.

"Mr. Close?"

"Yes."

"I have a position to fill that requires JDBC and Java Beans. Do you have that in your skill set?"

"Yes I do. Excuse me, though, what company are you calling from?"

"I'm calling from Respect You in the Morning Enterprises. We're a consulting and outplacement firm. You said you have JDBC and Java Beans?"

"Yes."

"What about Microsoft Project?"

"Yes."

"And Netscape?"

"Yes."

"Version 6.1?"

"Yes." At this point I started laughing to myself. The "skills" he mentioned were very specific tools and gave a narrow picture of my experience. He mentioned them in no particular order and he probably didn't know what any of them were. By then I knew he was one of those recruiters who just liked me because of my cute skill set and didn't care if I had a nice personality.

He might ask a few more questions about other skills, checking off my answers on his list as he went, and humming "Why Don't We Do It In The Road".

"Mr. Close, you've been looking for work?"

"Yes I have," I answered.

"Where have you been looking?"

"Job websites. This and that. The usual." This seemed like an odd question.

"Could you give me a list of the jobs you've applied for?"

"What?" I said.

"The other jobs you've applied for. It would help to know."

I could only guess that he was asking so that he didn't get himself into some kind of bidding contest with another recruiting firm. Understandable, but the question crossed the line.

"I'm sorry," I said. "That information is confidential." I thought, would you also like to know my weight and cup size?

"Listen, it's important for our files."

I said, "I understand that. But my job search is personal and I don't divulge it to others."

"Look, I thought we were partners here. I can't help you if you don't help me."

"Sorry," I said.

"So where do you want to go from here?"

"I think you and I should part ways. Good luck in your search."

"Okay. Good luck to you."

And I am glad to have his wish for luck. Luck is a good thing to have while looking for a job, in addition to patience, persistence, and of course, one's standards. The right opportunity will come when it's ready. In the meantime my heart will go on.

Charlie's First Day of Work

I work for a technology consulting company that, on the one hand, seeks to advise customers how best to use technology to advance their business goals, and secondly, works to provide first-rate people to carry out their decisions. This usually takes the form of building, improving, or maintaining software systems.

For my first assignment I was dispatched to the Information Technology department of our biggest client, BonzoCom, a large subsidiary of an even larger parent company. I went to join the team of software developers already stationed there. I arrived at nine on Monday morning and met the engagement manager, an employee of my company named Earl.

It had been several years since I had spent any time with a company this big. Recently I had worked at a startup software company so small that it was possible for a photographer to fit a picture of the whole company in one frame and still see all the faces.

BonzoCom was different. It was located in several interconnected one-story buildings so that if I stood at any intersection of any building I could see rows of cubicles stretching to the horizon in all directions like taupe wheat fields under a thousand fluorescent suns. In moving from one intersection to another, or one building to another, the location would change but the view would not. When I first walked into BonzoCom the sight of it gave me a stomach-dropping Hindu moment of realization. I was but a grain of sand on an enormous beach, and BonzoCom was itself only a grain of sand on an even greater beach, and so on *ad infinitum*.

Earl spent an hour with me and explained the project and the organizational landscape of BonzoCom. He gave me two binders full of documents to read. Some of the documents described the company's technology standards and procedures and others described the project we were working on. They taught me what I would be doing and the environment in which I would be doing it. It was a good assignment for a first day.

Earl said he had to leave to take care of other business, and that he would work on new employee administrative tasks for me, like getting me a badge, a computer, and a network login. I said thank you, and he said good-bye.

I spent the morning reading the first binder one page at a time, working to make the pages on the right side move to the left side.

I have to admit, sometimes my attention drifted. I imagined the contents of this binder were only an excerpt from an even larger binder, and that the larger binder made up only one page of an even larger binder, and so on until the last page of the world. Then I would snap back and return to reading this one page of this one binder until I could flip it over to the next page.

I was reading in Earl's office - actually a large open space enclosed by cubicle walls. His computer sat at one end and a teammate of mine worked on the other end. Her name was Jane and she was working quietly on some code, revising it, I presumed, in accordance with some of the documents I was reading. I exchanged a pleasant hello with her, and she with me, and we continued to work on our respective tasks.

I finished most of the reading early in the afternoon, before Earl returned from his other duties, so I went to his computer to do some related reading. The documents I had read referred to the website for the technology department of the parent corporation. I went to look at the site to get a broader view of what, I must say, was already a pretty darn broad view.

Earl had given me permission to work on his computer and a login to use. I turned to the computer, intending to spend the remainder of the day looking around on the corporate network and learning what I could learn.

It was the last completely peaceful moment of the day.

Jane, it so happened, was having technical difficulties, something or other about logins and printers. She called technical support to help her with her printing problem. She had logged in as ADMIN and couldn't print any documents, and she was tired of logging out of ADMIN and logging into TEMP just to print, and logging back into ADMIN to continue working. She wanted a support technician to fix whatever needed to be fixed so that ADMIN could send documents to the printer across the hallway.

Edith was dispatched from technical support to help Jane. Jane described her problem, and as soon as she got to the part about the ADMIN account Edith had something to say.

Edith explained that the ADMIN account was not intended for printing, not ever.

Jane tried to explain how she was just trying to have one login that could do both tasks and that -

Edith stopped Jane. Hearing that her original message had not been received, Edith sought to clarify it by repeating it a little louder and pointing at the computer. ADMIN is not for printing. If you have another account that can print you should use it instead.

That was when Jane tried to explain that she did have another account, but that she could not use the database with it...

So you should use *that* account, said Edith. How, Edith wanted to know, did Jane have the ADMIN password in the first place?

Jane answered that a coworker had given it to her.

Which one, asked Edith. She turned to me. Do you know anything about this?

First day! I chirped, raising my hand to swear and shaking my head no.

Jane told Edith that Evan had given her the account. Evan was another member of our team and not in the office that day.

Edith thought to herself out loud, Hmmm, she would have to have a talk with Evan. She said she was going to close out this support call - there was nothing she could do. Edith leaned in toward Jane and said, you can't print with ADMIN. You shouldn't even *have* ADMIN. I'm going to go change the password for ADMIN right now.

Edith turned to walk away, but Jane stopped her. Don't change the password, said Jane. The version of the database I'm using needs to have ADMIN.

What version, Edith wanted to know.

Version 9, said Jane.

This got Edith's attention in a big way. She explained in a penetrating fashion that BonzoCom did not support the use of Version 9, only Version 8. It didn't matter if Jane wanted to use Version 9, she Would Have To Get Approval to use it. BonzoCom didn't care what Jane thought was easier. Using non-approved software, Edith elaborated, could result in dismissal.

By this time Jane thought she had already gotten as much help from this technical support visit as she was going to get and told Edith thanks for her time. Edith withdrew her index finger and went on to her next call.

Jane turned back to her computer. She didn't say anything, but I think I saw her shoulder blades rise just a little bit.

I returned to reading, amused in a detached sort of way at how little things like network logins and database versions can get in the way of doing useful work. Ah, the vagaries of corporate life! I felt a haiku coming on.

> printer that prints not.
> support quickly sees the real
> problem: wrong database

No, I thought, eighteen is not the correct number of syllables. But never mind that now. It was time to learn more about the BonzoCom's software development methodology, version 8.1.6.

Which is what I was doing when I received a visit from Ted, another member of the team.

Ted explained to me that the people in the network security group had seen the activity on the computer I was using and knew that it was not Earl. This had caused some alarm, he said.

I nodded and told Ted I was using the computer and login Earl had given me. I said I was sorry if this had caused any concern. I believed that Earl was currently in the process of getting me a login but that it would take some time to arrange.

Ted said he understood, but that nevertheless it would be necessary for me to log out of the computer and not use it anymore until I had received proper credentials. The same, he said, applied to Jane, who was only using a temporary account.

By this time Jane had left for an appointment and was not present to hear this news.

Okay, I said. No problem. I logged out and Ted thanked me for understanding.

By that time it was late afternoon. I was able to make a little more progress by finding a few more printed documents to read. After that, I decided, I had learned enough for one day and went home.

I spoke to Earl by phone the next morning before work, and he said he needed to work on arranging to have accounts set up, and there was no point in coming to BonzoCom until it was done. He recommended I call the main office of my company and do whatever work they asked.

I found out later that, according to the way accounting works at BonzoCom, just putting me to work would incur a one-time setup cost of $10,000 to pay for getting me a computer, a badge, and sundry administration.

$10,000 - not bad! My presence makes the wheels turn.

That is, $10,000 is what I would have been worth if I were sitting at a desk at BonzoCom. Currently I'm sitting at home. Administrative startup costs here are low, about the price of one of Kathy's delicious homemade mochas.

The problem, I was told, was that Earl needed to find a manager ready to spend the money to put my cost on his budget. I offered to stay at home for a discounted rate of $5,000. The offer was not accepted and the needed manager has not been found, so I've continued to work from home.

Which is where I have been for the last week. Since the day with BonzoCom I have spent most of the time giving technical interviews to other potential candidates for my company.

I've conducted the interviews over the phone, where I've gotten to sit out on the front porch on a summer evening. Never mind the chirping of crickets, or the cat meowing through the open window, or the whistling wind, or the clanging of the wind chimes hanging from the deck above the porch. All the noise was a small price to pay for the chance to work outside.

Kathy heard me conducting the interview, sitting at the dining room table a few feet away from the window. When I came back in she made her voice deeper and more formal to imitate me: "Can you tell me the most recent project where you have used Java?"

"You heard me?" I said.

"Yep," answered Kathy.

I said, "I always like to ask people what specific experience they've had with a technology."

"Yeah, I know."

There was silence for a moment. Then she said, "You know what he probably said... I bet he said, 'I tried to have experience with Java but the suits at the office wouldn't let me!'"

"Ah, yes," I laughed. "That's exactly what he said. I told my boss he would fit right in and we should hire him."

"That's good. Your company will have more people to give interviews."

"That's right," I said. "You can't beat that."

Horse

I've been playing a lot of basketball since I arrived in Michigan. Kathy's brother Butch has a hoop in his back yard, and we play horse with his two oldest daughters.

Horse is a simple game, but even so, people bring different styles to it. My own style is conservative. I only shoot the shots I think I can make. I know if I can make 51% of my shots and I'm patient, I will beat anyone who can make only 49%.

I learned this approach from my father when I was still living at home. I practiced hard and gained confidence in my 10-foot jump shot, and after awhile I decided I was ready to drain a few on my dad.

"Rack 'em up," I shouted. "It's horse time!"

Dad was sitting in his easy chair, reading a book and watching *American Sportsman* on TV.

"Okay." He put a bookmark in his book, set it down, and we went out to the court in our driveway.

"You start," Dad said. I could tell he was serious because he had put on his headband.

I led off with a couple quick dribbles and swished a 12-footer through the net. I didn't look up because I knew I wouldn't be able to keep the grin off my face if I did. I just stepped away.

Dad took the ball out of the net over to the place where I had shot. He eyed it up, and without dribbling he tossed the ball up. It bounced twice on the rim and fell in. Lucky shot.

I made a couple more jumpers, and Dad matched them, but eventually I missed. It was his turn to shoot.

I thought he would take it out to twenty feet and hoist up a buzzer-beater, which would have bothered me because my own accuracy dropped off steeply after about fifteen feet. But he didn't. He went to the left block, three feet from the basket, and swung in a reverse lay-up, bouncing the ball off the right half of the backboard and into the basket, no rim. He caught the ball and threw a gentle bounce pass back to me.

A shot so close to the basket didn't look like it could be hard to make. I stepped over to the block. "From here, right?" I asked.

"Yep."

The basket was practically over my head, so close in fact that it was hard to tell exactly where it was. The rim was black because the sun was shining down on it. Should I lead off with my left foot or my right, take one dribble or two? How should I know? Why would I ever practice an easy shot like this one? I started off, deciding to take two dribbles but getting in only one before I lost control of the ball while trying to keep my eye on the basket. I recovered the ball and threw up a shot that clanged off the side of the rim.

"That's H," Dad said.

I didn't know it yet, but I had already taken the last shot of my own choosing. Dad ran the table, getting me to miss on a reverse lay-up from the other side (O), a left-handed bank shot while standing directly under the rim (R), a hook shot from five feet out (S), and a free throw (E). The free throw was actually my kind of shot, but I found it harder to make when the game was on the line.

"Go best two out of three?" Dad asked.

"No problem," I said, chest-passing the ball back to him. The next two were mostly the same. I won the second S to E and lost the third. Dad's pattern didn't change. Every shot was taken starting with his back to the basket, every shot was from close range, and every shot required more than I could muster of what I later learned to call footwork.

"Nice game, Son," he said at the end. He took his headband off and wiped his forehead with his sleeve. He didn't look up as we walked back into the kitchen.

It was the horse version of the tortoise and the hare. Or perhaps the ant and the grasshopper fits better, as in,

"Grasshopper, when Number One Son thinks he can play, Father say, 'It's winning time.'"

While I still don't care for reverse lay-ups, that experience taught me to stay within my own game. Winning at horse starts with shooting shots you can make.

Butch, on the other hand, prefers a more high-risk, high-reward style. If you prove you can make a shot from ten feet, he tries one from twenty. Can Butch himself make a twenty-footer? Only one way to find out - shoot the mother!

He also likes the fancy shots. We had a cookout at his house the other day, and he had parked his flatbed truck on the same cement where the hoop was. We played some horse, and Butch got up on the back of the truck, held onto the roof for support, twisted his body to face the basket, and shot the ball with the other hand.

Clang! The ball bounced off the rim and into the bushes.

Me, I shot a five-foot baseline jumper, and it went in.

Butch tried the truck shot eight more times and finally made one. I tried it and missed. "That's a letter for me," I said. If memory serves, and it does, I won that game.

In the next game Butch said, "Okay, you have to make it with your shirt over your head, whistling show tunes."

"Oh, sure," I said, "fat chance." But I'll be darned if Butch didn't make that one.

"*Sound Of Music* good enough for you?" I asked.

"I don't care. Just shoot it."

My belly is still sunburned from having my shirt over my head while trying to pucker long enough to whistle. My shot fell short...and wide, and "My Favorite Things" is in a bad key for me. That's H, har-dee-har-har.

Butch's oldest daughters, Samantha and Robin, play too, although they're still a little young. We bring the basket down to about seven feet and they shoot shots from four feet or closer. Those are the shots they can make, so they stick to those. The problem is that from that range Butch and I can both hold the ball over the rim and drop it in standing flat-footed. It made for a good field goal percentage to do it that way.

Butch wasn't satisfied just to drop the ball in. He dunked the ball and swung from the rim. "Slamma jamma!" he yelled.

His girls thought that wasn't fair. *"Dad!"* they cried.

But they shouldn't get discouraged. If they keep practicing, it's only a matter of time before they learn to drain some jumpers.

I've also been playing with Kendall, the daughter of Kathy's friend Wendy. Kendall is nine years old, just over four feet tall, and a jock. Soccer is her real sport, but there are no summer soccer camps around, so she slums around by shooting baskets with me. She recently signed up for a basketball camp, mainly to keep one of her friends company.

After her second day at camp we went to shoot some baskets at the local schoolyard. She showed me drills she had been working on.

"Lay-ups..."

"That's good," I said.

"...shooting, and dribbling, and passing, and running," she said.

Her favorite part was the running. She showed me several running drills: up and down, side to side, wind sprints, up and down then side to side then up and down, and so on.

We practiced shooting. She worked on the run-stop-and-pop from eight feet that she had learned at camp, and I worked on my hook shot. A big man needs a hook if he wants to dominate in the paint.

She said, "You want to play a game?"

"Sure," I said.

"Okay - whoever is first to make it five times wins."

It was a simple game, even simpler than horse. You make it, you get a point, and you don't have to try to make the other player's shot. I shot my hook, she shot her short jumper from straight on, and I won the first game 5-2.

"Go best two out of three?" I said.

"Sure."

The hook started going cold while her shot started to go down. In a real game I could compensate for weak offense with rebounding, defense, and doing the little things that help a team win. In this game, however, I was just plain losing. She took it 5-3.

"Okay," I said. "This one is for tonight's championship. No pressure."

"Whoever wins gets..." she paused, thinking, "...gets to drink first. Okay?" It was a hot evening and we had both brought water bottles.

"Okay," I said. I thought, that's quite a prize. Maybe we could call it the Dixie Cup.

It was her night. When she went up 3-2 and it was my turn she said, "Bring it on!" I tried, but the basket was only getting smaller.

When she was up 4-3 and it was her turn to shoot she said, "How about if we say the loser has to run from there to over there and back...three times." Her arm swept across the length of the parking lot.

"I like the drinking water thing better," I told her. "Don't get fancy. Just make your shot."

"Okay." And she made her shot. Game, set, and match. Kendall won two games to one.

We both moved to our water bottles and Kendall stooped to pick hers up. She said, "You have to wait."

"Okay," I said.

She took a long pull that lasted about thirty seconds. "Wait," she said. "I'm not done."

"Okay," I said.

She took a second long drink, this time almost emptying her bottle. "Okay," she said, looking at me.

"May I drink now?"

"Yes."

"Okay, good game."

"Thanks."

And before we went back to Wendy's house Kendall ran from there to over there and back, doing all the running drills she had learned.

Some people just like to run.

Lightning Drive

Seattle, where I lived for many years, is known for its rain. Other places have snowfall in winter, but Seattle has rain. Where they have showers in the spring and fall, Seattle has that and still more rain.

I used to take walks in it when I was younger, and I would not feel satisfied until I came home soaked through and drops of water poured down the back of my neck. What most people feel about the sun, I feel about the rain.

Then Kathy came from Michigan to live with me, and I didn't spend as much time with the rain as before. I was older and there were other things to do. We stayed indoors and built our life together.

In Seattle, the rain is almost always polite and muted, a little like Seattle itself. Peaceful.

Later we moved back to Michigan to be with Kathy's family and I learned there is rain here too. Michigan rain, however, is very different, as I found out on the way home from a family cookout at the house of Kathy's sister Marti.

The meal was full of burgers and bratwurst and family gathered elbow to elbow around a small picnic table. There was constant passing of meats and condiments with bursts of eating thrown in.

I was the center of attention for the young daughters of Kathy's brother Butch. They are almost, but not quite, too big to treat Uncle Charlie like an amusement park ride. Ellie demanded "Spin me!" in her cutest and loudest voice, and once the spinning started, her older sisters Samantha and Robin wanted spins too. Could I say, "Sorry, you're too big"? No, I couldn't say it. Next time they might really be too grown up to spin.

There was only so much Uncle Charlie to go around. I used to think I knew how hard it can be to treat others fairly, but that was before I tried to make sure my excited and crafty nieces got the same number of spins.

Marti asked me not to let the girls back onto the white carpet with their dirty bare feet, so I wetted down a beach towel and washed and dried every foot. As I finished each niece I said, solemnly, "Go inside." Sweat rolled down my back by the time I was done.

The nieces left with their father before the rain started. The clouds turned black and rain crashed down. There was nothing polite about this rain. In Michigan, summer rain isn't just rain. It's thunder and lightning too, much louder, brighter and more dangerous than it ever was in Seattle. Kathy, Marti, and I remained safe inside the house and talked about one thing and another while waiting for the storm to calm down.

Marti was trying to sell the house she owned with her closest friend of the last ten years. The friend was bankrupt and already owed Marti money that she might never repay, and Marti badly wanted to get onto the next stage of her life.

Butch didn't get along with the owner's son of his last job. He got into a chest poking match with him, and now he was out of work.

And there was a third sister who was almost never mentioned at family gatherings and who remained nameless here.

Sometimes it is so clear to me that all it would take is one bad decision or a little bad luck in my life, or the lives of my new family, to turn comedy to tragedy, and if it does there is nowhere for me to hide from it.

After awhile we thought the rain had settled down enough to risk going home.

The lull in the weather was only temporary and the drive home strained my nerves. I swerved the car in and out between the deep patches of standing water on Atherton Road and showers of spray were thrown up from the wheels of oncoming cars. I drove slowly and hung on when the car tried to skid off the road.

But the water wasn't as bad as the lightning. It flashed ahead of us brightly enough to make us blink. Was it beautiful or was it going to kill us? I hoped it would strike somewhere else and I could not take my eyes off it.

We pulled up to the house and rushed inside through the downpour, glad to be out of the car and back inside where it was warm and dry. I shook water out of my hair while Kathy phoned Marti to tell her we were safe.

wide open road
in a rainstorm
the dazzle of lightning

Liverpool

Kathy and her sister Marti love to play cards. Their mother was a fanatic card player herself and taught her daughters at an early age. Kathy's grandmother also played cards, and I bet Kathy could trace her mothers all the way back to the old country in central Europe. It wouldn't shock me to learn that her great-great-great-great grandmother played bridge with the Holy Roman Emperor and won most of the time.

Playing cards was one of the things Kathy gave up when she came to live with me. I'm tone deaf with cards. They don't interest me and I don't understand them, so Kathy and I almost never played. She must have felt like she was stuck on a desert island the eight years she lived in Seattle. She had an ocean view and all the coconuts she could eat, but there was no one to play Hearts. Marti must have felt the same way. Having given her sister up to the uncultured brute from the West, she lived without cards and her soulmate to play them with.

During her years in Seattle the bond between sisters was stretched but not severed. When Kathy moved back to Michigan, the card playing resumed where it had left off.

Their favorite game is Liverpool, a rummy-style game they've played all their lives, and which, now that they are reunited, they play almost every weekend. They always invite me, and when I am feeling in good spirits, I accept.

I am not in their league, but I can appreciate them even if I cannot compete with them. There are a hundred things that they do easily that make me feel like I'm learning to read for the first time. C-A-T spells "cat".

I usually sit between Kathy and Marti so that Kathy discards to me and I discard to Marti. Marti, being the player on my left, and for the good of us all, usually deals the first hand. For the next hand, the deal continues away from me to Kathy.

First hand: two books, ten cards. Everyone gets their cards and begins to organize them by card value, twos with twos, queens with queens, and so on. Marti and Kathy finish in about four seconds. For me...well, keep reading and I'll tell you when I'm finished.

The rhythm of draw and discard begins. It has a unique sound. Imagine a three-legged animal walking down a sidewalk. Flick-pat, flick-pat, flick-pat. Flick-pat, flick-pat, flick-pat. Now imagine the creature has lost one of its legs in an accident and that it was replaced by a prosthetics doctor who makes heavy wooden furniture in his spare time. Flick-pat, flick-pat, ...thunk-BANG. Flick-pat, flick-pat, ...thunk-BANG.

I am that third leg. I think long and hard before I draw. I look long and hard at the cards in my hand and the card I've drawn. I think long and hard about what I am going to do. I take a long time doing it.

Is it the right thing?

Is it the best thing?

Thunk-BANG.

Part of the problem is the physical act of holding the cards. They are slippery and I have a hard time holding them so I can see them all at once. Marti and Kathy do not have this problem. They hold their cards spaced evenly apart with German precision and the dexterity of a geisha with her bamboo fan.

The other problem is mental: what to do with the cards? When the hand is like the first hand - all books - or like the seventh hand - all runs - it's not as difficult. I can get my mind around one thing: get cards that fit in with the pattern. The hands like the second (one book, one run), the fifth (two books, one run), and the sixth (one book, two runs) give me the most trouble. Each card could potentially play in a book or a run, or both, and the best place to play it can shift with the addition of new cards. Picture trying to play a violin while riding a bicycle and you can get a glimmer of how awkward it is for me.

So far I've described what can be called the offensive side of the game - working on your own hand to get the cards you need. There is also a defensive side. The cards you think are trash may be treasure to the player on your left. It therefore behooves you to watch what your opponents pick up and what they throw away. You don't want to throw out cards another player can use.

Kathy is a master of this. If I throw away a king, she starts discarding all kings as well as aces and queens of the same suit, confident that I can't use them.

This is beyond me most of the time. I am too busy pedaling my bike and tuning the violin to look for oncoming traffic. *Pizz, pizz, pizz...*

Most of the time Kathy knows my hand better than I know it myself. When Marti discards a card that Kathy knows I need, she hesitates before drawing.

I look up. "What?"

"Do you want to buy that?" Kathy asks.

"Um..." I say. I try to sound like I'm considering my options carefully, but mostly I'm trying to comprehend my own cards. "Ah, yes I will buy that. Give it here, please!"

Kathy isn't fooled by my bravado. She hands me the card and winks.

And play proceeds. The best thing for me about playing Liverpool is that time passes as I study my cards, and it is always my turn.

I look up. "What?"

"It's your turn, honey."

"Okay."

I look up. "What?"

"It's your turn, honey."

"Okay." Thunk-BANG.

I have, however, learned some defensive strategy. First, I avoid face cards and aces as much as possible. My ideal hand consists of nothing but five-point cards. Why? Because there is a good chance I won't get to go down, and a fist full of low cards is a lot better to get caught with than a bunch of ten-point royalty. I've had to learn this the hard way.

Kathy throws down her last card. Zero points for her. She's keeping the scorecard, so she says, "Marti?"

"Fifteen."

"Charlie?"

"What?"

"How many points have you got, hon?"

Counting... "Um...two hundred forty-five."

"Couldn't get the jack, eh?"

"No."

"That's because I had it right here," she says, picking it up from the pile in front of her and showing it to me.

"Right..."

The second defensive trick I've learned is to look twice before discarding when other people have already laid down. More than once I have earned two penalty cards when I missed the fact that my discard plays on someone else's hand. It's like touching an electric fence that I didn't know was there, and now that I've felt its sting, I discard very, very carefully.

But enough about Charlie the novice. The real game takes place on a higher plane between Kathy and Marti. I'll describe a game I watched but didn't play so that you can hear the language in its purest form.

"Nice deal, Mart," says Kathy. "I've got nothing."

Marti shrugs.

Flip-pat. Flip-pat.

"I thought you were looking for that." Kathy holds up a card from her hand so Marti can see it.

Marti holds up a card from her own hand and lifts an eyebrow.

"Ah-ha!" says Kathy.

Flip-pat. Flip-pat.

"The nine, eh. Going to draw inside?"

Shrug. "Maybe."

"You want to buy that?"

"No, I've already got the six. But thank you."

"No, thank you."

"No, thank *you.*"

Flip-pat. Flip-pat.

"Here you go. I know you want it but I can't give you anything else."

"Cool!"

"Going down?"

"Not yet. I need one more card."

"Club?"

"Spade."

"Ha!"

Flip-pat. Marti goes down with ten cards plus six more she's bought. After discarding she has only one more card to play.

"Well now I know who had the low diamonds."

"Tee-hee."

Kathy goes down, throws two of her cards onto Marti's cards, and has only two cards left to play.

Flip-pat. "Crap!" This wasn't the card Kathy wanted.

Flip-pat. Sigh. It wasn't Marti's card either.

Flip-pat. "Crap!"

Flip-pat. Sigh.

And so on, Crap-sigh, crap-sigh, like the last ninety-six bars of a Beethoven symphony, until at last the cards begin to fall. Marti draws a card that plays on Kathy and she discards the last card in her hand.

"Ohhhh crap!" says Kathy, and the conductor turns to face the audience's applause. "Ten points for me. Forty-five to sixty." She writes down her score, shuffles the cards, and begins to deal the next hand.

Okay...*now* I'm finished organizing my cards.

Dunkin' the Barbarian

In Seattle people take their coffee seriously. They know the difference between good coffee and bad, and avoid the bad. Coffee is a like a family pet, accepted and known for its own personality. Coffee is embraced in Seattle the way wine is in Bordeaux or oil in Houston.

Not so in Michigan. Here they have other totems. Coffee isn't culture here. It isn't identity. It's just coffee. Everyone drinks it and no one cares.

Yet I care. Even though my home sits in the middle of Michigan, I think of it as sovereign Seattle territory, like an embassy, or better yet a beacon. It lets Michigan in and it also projects Seattle out.

The other day Kathy's brother Butch came to visit. He had stopped at Dunkin' Donuts for coffee on the way to our place. I first saw the sugar-frosted Styrofoam cup as he walked in the door, holding it at arm's length while he kicked off his shoes.

"What's *that?*" I asked, knowing perfectly well what it was.

"What?"

"What are you holding there, in your hand?"

"A doorknob?"

"The *other* hand," I said.

"Oh. It's coffee."

"Dunkin' Donuts?"

"Yeah."

"*DUN*-kin' *DO*-nuts!"

"Yeah, Bro. It's good. You want some?" He held out the cup to me.

I held up my hands, palms out. "No thank you." I turned my head back, hands still raised. "Kathy? Do we have some of our coffee left for Mr. Butch over here?"

She said, "Yes, unless you drank it all."

"That's okay," Butch said. "I'm good." I could see through the Styrofoam that the cup was almost full.

"Kathy, would you help him please?" I said, waving Kathy around. "Butch?"

Butch didn't hear me. He had torn open the perforated hole in the plastic lid and was drinking.

"Butch!"

"Yeah?"

"Kathy is going to get you some of our coffee. I want you to drink it, okay?"

"All right. Whatever."

Kathy walked Butch over to the counter. She pulled down the cream and sugar and a porcelain cup, and showed him the coffee carafe filled with Starbucks House Blend that had been brewed less than an hour earlier.

Butch mixed it the way he liked it and took a drink. He jerked his head back and shook it. "This is strong!"

"Yeah, sure is," I said. "Good, isn't it?"

"Yeah, I guess."

"Go ahead. Drink some more."

I made the old coffee disappear while Kathy invited Butch to come drink his fresh coffee out on the porch. He drank carefully at first, then with unforced enjoyment.

He was content, and so was I. Family, good coffee, summer morning sunlight. It was a small thing, but it's moments like this when you think you can make a difference in the world.

Halloween Party

I've been working away at a software project since the end of September. It has gone well. We have nearly finished the first phase of the project and the results look good.

But - do I even need to say this? - the project has taken a lot of work and not everything has gone as smoothly as expected.

I have a theory that software engineers actually work for free, like sales people working on straight commission, and that an engineer starts earning a living only when he says "I don't know." Either, "I don't know how to do that and I will figure it out," or "It was working before and I don't know why it isn't working now."

Any work that an engineer does that isn't driven by "I don't know" is ordinary work that can be scheduled into a forty-hour week, and any work that starts with "I don't know" has the potential to be open-ended and difficult.

We've had quite a few I-don't-knows on my project, starting with everyone learning to use at least two software tools he had never worked with before. "How do I use them?" everyone asked, and we each answered, "I don't know but we'll figure it out."

The tool that drew the most attention was a thing called Flash. Even if you don't know what Flash is, you have probably seen it. If you've ever watched an animated advertisement in a web page, chances are it used Flash. Flash gives a web designer the ability to add visually striking effects to a web page, and it can also be used for more productive tasks, like transmitting and receiving information over the Internet.

Our project was seven weeks long, and in the fourth week, before any web pages had actually been built, the team decided it would be "easier", and the customer decided it would be "slicker", to use Flash instead of traditional techniques for some aspects of the web pages.

How could we use Flash to achieve these goals with less effort and more pizzazz? Only one of us had ever worked with Flash before, which, as a point of departure, was actually better than average. We said, "We don't know, and we'll figure it out."

It turned out that learning Flash was a little bit like a walking through a swamp: easy to get in but hard to get out. Two members of the team waded for days through the bog, first as they struggled to use Flash at all, then as they fought with each other over how to use it best. The team, which in theory had three engineers, in reality had only me and a largely-invisible clump called "Working on Flash". Wally, the executive of my company who stood either to make or lose money on the project, questioned the wisdom, to put it mildly, of adopting Flash halfway through the project, and tensions began to rise just a little bit.

Flash wasn't the only bump in the road. There were others. We found out the hard way that the computers we used to write the software were different from the ones the customers used. For example, our computers had the ability to draw images on the screen, and by images I mean anything visual at all, like a picture of a tree or even the letter "F". I spent a long, tiring day trying to figure out why the software worked on my computer but not the customer's until I finally became desperate and read the section of the manual that described this exact problem and implemented the solution it recommended.

Everything came out well in the end. The two members of the team figured out how to use Flash and the results justified the time and effort spent, and the customer was as impressed as we expected he would be.

That was the kind of week it was and that is the kind of project it had been. Successful, rewarding, educational and uphill almost every step of the way.

That week, it so happened, ended with Halloween on Friday.

You thought I had forgotten I was supposed to be writing about Halloween? I did not forget. I only wanted you to understand the wrung-out state I was in when Halloween arrived.

Kathy's friend Wendy invited Kathy and me to her Halloween party and gave us the job of handing out candy to the kids.

We live in a town small enough to organize its Halloween. The town air siren sounded at six o'clock to announce the beginning of trick-or-treating and it would sound again at eight o'clock to announce the end.

Wendy's daughter Kendall, dressed as a vampiress, set out trick-or-treating with her dad Carl.

Wendy, Kathy, and I stationed ourselves on the porch at six , each holding a bucket of candy. Fortunately Wendy's candy choices did not include my personal favorites, so I was able to give it all away. The stereo in the living room played "Monster Mash" and "Werewolves of London" through the open doorway.

The kids appeared from nowhere at the sound of the siren and I had so much fun. I had not handed out candy at Halloween in maybe...well maybe not ever. Most of the kids over eight years old were veterans. They knew how to walk up, say trick-or-treat, accept the candy, say thank-you, and soldier on. Kathy and I threw candy in every bowl and bag. We handed it out like a politician gives out handshakes at a barbecue.

"Trick-or-treat," said the boy or girl.

"Trick-or-treat," said I, and dropped Milk Duds into the outstretched sack.

And so on and so on. It had a soothing ritual-like quality to it. I imagined we were doing this in Japan, bowing with pressed hands and staccato intonations of supplication and generosity. Surely, I thought, sumo wrestlers would like Milk Duds.

Not all of the children were experienced. Many were barely more than babies who crawled up the porch steps to get their first candy. I sat like a Buddha waiting for the penitent to arrive. "What do you say, Joshua?" the parent would ask. "What do you say, Megan?" The babies did not know what to say, and would not have been able to say it anyway with their fingers in their mouths.

And then there were the old-timers, the kids who had been trick-or-treating for almost half their lives.

"Trick-or-treat!" said the boy. His voice was friendly but had a little too much bass in it.

"Trick-or-treat," said I, looking through the bowl for a razor. A shaving razor, that is, not an eating razor.

Every once in a while there was a child who held the bag out just a little longer than necessary in the hope that I would throw in a second treat. Ah, that moment of tension. I was cruel and filled that moment with the sound of no-candy. "One's enough," I'd say.

Wendy mixed drinks while Kathy and I gave out treats. Screwdrivers, I can say from experience, are excellent for trick-or-treating. The children don't know what they're missing.

The street filled with the procession of children and parents dressed in costume and marching from house to house, and at eight o'clock the end-of-Halloween siren sounded and people started to drift back home.

That's when the kids' party stopped and the adults' party

began. Wendy had invited several of her friends over for drinks, cake, and gossiping.

Me, I wasn't sure where I would fit in with all the ladies, so I stayed outside. Kendall had a basketball hoop set up in the driveway. I got out the ball and started shooting. It was already dark outside, but the floodlights on the side of the house provided enough light to see the basket.

Before long Kendall and Cody, the next door neighbor boy, got back from trick-or-treating and joined in with the basketball. Then Kendall's friend Heather showed up wearing a long blue gown. She could have been a gypsy, or maybe a princess. Whatever she was, the gown didn't stop her. She wanted to play basketball and she was the tallest person on the court except for me.

Before long, Carl, Cody's dad John, and Heather's dad Pete were leaning against the tailgate of Carl's pickup truck, drinking beer and watching.

So we played ball, Kendall and Heather on one team and Cody and I on the other. I guarded Heather since she was closest to my height. I threw an elbow into her arm at the start of the game – you know, just to show her I was going to play defense. She threw one back, *hard*, to tell me she was going to play offense.

It turned out that Heather could play bigger than her size. She was fast, ran hard for the ball, and could shoot. She made it difficult for me. If I played her like she was a kid she would out-fierce me. If I played her like she was a grown-up, I would have to knock her to the deck. And she left no choices in-between. I could scare most of the other kids with my size, but not her. Well, I got a little squeamish about playing my hardest and she scored several baskets on me.

We actually got to play some ball for a few minutes. There wasn't a lot of passing or teamwork, and there was too much shooting, but it was a real game.

Slowly more parents arrived for the party, and so did more

kids. A hard moment came for me when a third friend of Kendall's arrived and wanted to play. I did my duty and bowed out of the game to make room for the new boy. Basketball was for the kids, not the grownups. Yep.

By the time five or six kids were playing, all sense of organization was lost. Someone got out a second ball and began to shoot it. Boys started to showboat and compete over who got to be team captain. The dads let the kids sort it out for themselves.

Then the kids grew bored and all flocked across the street to the schoolyard. They hung out there, talking amongst themselves about I don't know what. Best for me not to know. The worst thing was they took both basketballs with them. I looked up at the basket and thought how empty it was.

But it did not stay empty for long. I walked over to the trunk of my car and pulled out the basketball I kept there for situations like these. Shot...swish!

I took a few shots and Pete jumped up from the tailgate, caught one of the rebounds and took his own shot. How long had he wanted to do that?

We played for a while: shoot, pass, shoot, pass. Then Heather joined us. Shoot, pass, shoot, pass. Oh yeah!

The other kids came back and Kendall had an idea. "Charlie, will you take us to the park? Please!"

I thought it sounded like fun until the grownup in me kicked in. I thought of eight pairs of parents who would have to approve, and I felt stuck. Um... Um...

"Come on! Let's go!"

I looked left and right. I shrugged. "Okay, let's go."

I walked with half a dozen kids to the park a block away, and we stopped at the giant gravel bed covered with tire swings and jungle gyms made from logs and stainless steel. "Stay where I can see you!" I called, which wasn't very far. It was dark by the jungle gyms, with only a couple of parking lot lights for illumination.

I got some exercise from pushing kids on tire swings -

higher! - but mostly I kept to the side and out of the way. My job was to be there but not be there.

When they got tired of climbing and swinging Kendall had another bright idea. "Charlie, can we go to the graveyard, please!" There was a cemetery a block away from the park.

Well, if you can't walk through a graveyard on Halloween night, when can you? "Sure," I said. "Who wants to go?"

A couple of the kids didn't want to go. I asked them to go back to Wendy's house together and the rest of us went to the cemetery. Staying with me were Jason, Robert wearing the peace symbol from his neck, Cody, Katie in her black gown, her sister Libby in a tuxedo, Roxanne in blue flannel pajamas with a zip up front and padded feet, Rachel, and Kendall.

We walked out of the park through a hole in the chain link fence, up a side street, and along an iron fence until we found an entrance to the cemetery. As we entered I found out some of the kids were more excited than others about walking among the graves. Jason and Robert practically ran to get in.

But Roxanne started to get scared. "It's not respectful." She stood still and didn't want to move.

"It's okay," I told her. She was ten years old. How could I explain to her that the dead might not mind children walking among them? I said, "It's going to be fine."

One girl chanted, "Think about flowers! Think about flowers!"

We walked on through the dark and weaved our way between the stones. A dozen small feet: some running, some walking slowly, some tiptoeing. It was quiet except for the swishing of shoes through fallen leaves.

We walked past two open gates, still in the cemetery, and left through the third, which opened onto the street corner nearest to Wendy's house. As we exited, a car approached with its headlights on us. I stepped forward and saw that it was a police car. I walked up to the driver's side.

"Evening, officer," I said.

The officer was an older man with the town police department. He had gotten a report that kids were walking through the cemetery. When he saw who we were and that I was with them, there was no trouble. The kids surrounded the windows on the driver and passenger side. Half of them knew the officer and started talking with him, and he chatted us up and sent us on our way.

Jason and Robert got ahead of the group and broke into a run to Wendy's house. Me, I stayed with the others and took my time getting back.

The party was starting to wind down at Wendy's house, and most of the food had been eaten. We left a short time later, and as we were getting back in our car I said, "That...was...cool!"

"Did you have fun, honey?" Kathy asked.

"Yes I did," I said. "Yeah..."

Flowers

If anyone asks me, "What is the smartest thing you have ever done?" I will have an answer.

The surprising thing is that it has nothing to do with my job or any of my hobbies. I've done a few smart things, it's true, but nothing like this. The smartest thing I ever did is a story of true love and snatching victory from the jaws of defeat.

A few years ago, Kathy, my wife-to-be, was still living in Flint, Michigan and I was living in Seattle, Washington. We had already met, courted, fallen in love and decided we were going to be with each other. Kathy was trying to sell her house so she could move to Seattle.

Kathy had no interest in Seattle itself. She had lived her whole life in Michigan and would not have thought to move west if it weren't for me.

But not so for Kathy's little sister Marti. For some reason Seattle fascinated her and she wanted to live there. Maybe it was the hot music and culture scene, or maybe it was just because Seattle was not Flint. Marti had loved Seattle, or the idea of Seattle, for a long time.

She convinced her best friend Crystal to move there with her. They packed their things and boarded an Amtrak train. I met them at the station when they arrived and helped them get started in their new home. Kathy expected to join us all as soon as the house was sold, which could take weeks or even months.

Those are the facts, but the truth goes deeper. Kathy and Marti's parents both died within ten days of each other when Kathy was twenty-two and Marti was fifteen. Kathy raised Marti for the next ten years. They lived together, took care of each other, and are as close as two people can be. When Marti moved away Kathy wasn't just losing a roommate or a sister - she was sending her daughter out into the world for the first time.

The day Marti left, Kathy was still in the middle of packing as much of her house as she could, surrounded by shoulder-high piles of boxes.

Moving is always hard. It makes you look at the old possessions of your life and ask what they mean now. Moving is lonely work.

I knew all this was happening even though I was thousands of miles away, and I knew Kathy would feel sad and alone in her house that day.

I realized I could not do much, but I could send her some flowers to tell her I knew what she was going through and that I was thinking about her.

I was pleased with myself for having the idea. That, I thought, ought to register about a 9.8 on her you're-so-sweet-o-meter. And in hindsight I really was thoughtful, especially for a self-absorbed, never-knows-what-to-do, women-are-from-Venus dork like I was in those days.

I was so thoughtful that for days I didn't actually get around to ordering the flowers. Just knowing that I *would* send Kathy flowers to cheer her up was enough for me.

Well, time slipped away and I did not try to place an order until the day before they needed to arrive. I walked home from work a little faster that evening, and I could feel that I had not left much time.

I walked up to Johnny's Flowers. Even before I got there I could see it was closed. The time was 6:20 PM.

Uh-oh, I thought. No panic, no panic. There were two more shops up the street. I walk-galloped, gripping the straps of my book bag to keep it from bouncing on my back. I went to the first store, and to the second - both closed.

The walk back down to my apartment was long and slow, and my thoughts were dark and stormy. If I came up to a stone in my path, I kicked it.

But then, just as I passed the post office a block away from home, I had an idea and I started to gallop again.

I ran into the apartment, threw down my bag, and picked up the phone. I dialed Information.

"What city, please?"

"Honolulu!" I said.

"Go ahead," said the operator.

"Give me the names of three flower shops. I don't care which ones."

She took a moment and told me the names. I wrote them down. "Would you like me to connect you, sir?"

"Sure," I said. "To the first one. Thank-you."

"You're welcome, sir."

The phone began to ring with a tone that sounded a million miles away. A woman answered it. "Island Flowers. How may I help you?"

"Are you still open?" I demanded.

"Yes, sir, we are."

"Oh, that's great, because I'm calling from Seattle and we're two time zones ahead of you. Everything's already closed here."

"Well, we're open, sir. How can I help you?"

"I need you to send flowers to Flint, Michigan tomorrow. Can you do that?"

"Of course. What would you like?"

I placed the order, hung up the phone and threw both hands into the air. *"Yes!"*

I felt like I had just scored the winning goal at the Soccer World Cup. (Call me Rafael Pantanagua.) The announcer cried "Goooooooooooooooal!", and I ripped off my shirt and whirled it over my head as I took a victory lap around Estadio Nacional in front of 80,000 screaming fans. They could all see my small but very athletic torso. Some of them pulled off their shirts too.

I went to work the next day and I told everybody. And when I say everybody, I mean *everybody*. I told the story so many times that I honed it into a speech I could deliver from memory.

I said, "Did you know that Hawaii is two hours behind us in Seattle?" I told them about Marti coming here and how my girlfriend Kathy was sad and alone, and how I tried to send her flowers and screwed up, but that it turned out okay because of Hawaii.

Most of my coworkers listened politely. Some of them laughed, and some of them asked why I didn't just call FTD's toll free ordering number.

"Oh," I said. "Well, because I didn't know about that." To me it made the achievement even greater because I had had less to work with. Who is cleverer, the person who builds a house with a belt full of tools, or the one who builds it with his bare hands?

That's right. I thought so.

This, too, was before you could buy flowers on the Internet. Things were primitive in those days. All we had was the telephone.

But the best part of the day, better than telling the story to all my coworkers, was when the phone rang at my desk and it was Kathy.

"Hey, you," she said.

"Heeey," I said.

"Somebody just sent me some flowers. Some hunky guy. You know anything about that, Mister Charlie Close?"

"Well, maybe I do. Hunky guy, huh? What's he look like?"

"He's tall and handsome and he's got cute hair that looks all messed up in the morning, and he's very considerate..."

"He does sound hunky," I said.

"Yeah," said Kathy, trailing off...

Ladies and gentlemen, a call like this is what makes it all worth while. I was so happy.

Now the next thing I *wanted* to say was, "Did you know that Hawaii is two hours behind Seattle?..." Kathy would listen to anything I said now and think it was great. I came *this* close to telling her about the trick I had to pull off to get her flowers.

But I didn't, not that day. I told her instead that I knew she would be feeling sad and that I was thinking about her.

I used to think that calling Hawaii was the smartest thing I ever did. But now, if anyone ever asks me, I will tell them this -

I was smart enough, that one time, to shut up.

Blue is a Boy

"You think you know someone, and then they say something like that."

Kathy spoke those words to me the other day. Why? Because I just said what everyone knows.

"Blue is a boy color," I said.

"And what?" said Kathy. "Pink is for girls?"

"No, that's not what I mean. I'm not saying that blue is *for* boys. I'm saying that blue *is* a boy.

"What?"

"Blue is male, just like red is male and orange is female." I took a sip of coffee.

Kathy stared at me. "I don't get it."

"Get what?"

"Orange is female?"

"Yeah, sure." I shrugged. Of course it is.

"What about green?"

"Female."

"Yellow?"

"Male."

"Okay," she said. "*Why* is yellow male?"

"He just is. I didn't make him that way. He and green are the teenagers."

"Teenagers?"

"Sure. Red and orange are the parents, and yellow and green are their teenage children."

Now Kathy was intrigued.

"When did you figure that out?" she asked.

"Long time ago."

"Like...last *year?* Five years ago? When?" What she really wanted to know was if I figured it out after we met.

"No," I said, "a long, long time ago. Like when I was six. I've always known."

"And you never told me?"

"What is there to tell?"

Kathy squinted. "If red and orange are parents, what's blue?"

"A son, but younger, like five years old."

"Purple?"

"The baby of the family."

"Boy or girl?"

"Too young to tell. Could be either."

Kathy dropped her face into her hands. "Oh great."

"Didn't you know this?"

She looked back up. "No. Why would I come up with a stupid idea like that?"

"It's not an idea. It's the truth."

"Okay...what's pink? Girl or boy?"

"I don't know."

"What do you mean you don't know?"

"I only know the rainbow colors, not the fancy colors."

"So pink doesn't have a gender?"

"I'm sure it does," I said. "I just don't know what it is."

"Oh."

"Sorry."

"So you don't know sepia?"

"No."

"Chartreuse?"

"No."

"Mauve?"

I shrugged. "No. Sorry."

"Magenta?"

"I said no. Just the crayon colors."

"Burnt sienna?"

I sighed. "Just the eight color box, not the sixty-four."

"Oh."

Kathy paused to take this in. She mulled it over. She gave it some careful thought.

"You know," she said, "that is the dumbest thing I have ever heard, ever."

"Okay," I said. I didn't take offense. Why would I take offense for things being the way they are? Should I feel foolish that the sky is blue?

"Does anything else have gender that I don't know about?"

"No, nothing, except numbers of course."

Kathy's eyes widened. "Six."

"Female."

"No way!"

I shrugged. "What?"

"Seven?"

"Male."

"Thirteen?"

"Female."

"Why?"

"Because three is."

"What?"

"It only goes up to ten, then it repeats. Three is a girl, so thirteen is too."

"Oh. What's ten?"

"He's the king, along with Queen Nine."

"Kind of like red and orange?"

"Yes, except they aren't king and queen."

"Eight?"

"Princess."

"This is all starting to make sense," she said.

I smiled. "Cool."

"I mean, I figured out you're an idiot."

"You can say what you want, but King Ten is not mocked."

Pronoun Muteness

I believe I have identified a new medical condition that affects people living together. For example, when I am working in the living room, Kathy calls from the kitchen.

"...feed the dog!"

"What!" I say.

"Time for...to feed the dog!"

I am sure she did not speak the pronoun to indicate *who* should feed the dog. Is she saying that she is going to do it, or is she asking me to do it?

At this point I have a choice. I could seek clarification in order to apprehend her intent, or I could acknowledge her words without worrying too much about what she said.

Call it doing the right thing, or call it exaggerated politeness, or call it foolishness, I usually opt for asking what she means. "*What?* Who's going to feed the dog?"

"*You* are going to feed the dog!"

And that's the way it works almost every time. Did she say she wanted me to do it the first time, or did she switch her story after I asked her to repeat it? I may never know. What I do know is that I gave her an opportunity to delegate the task to me, and if I had remained quiet I might still be watching TV instead of scooping out Mighty Dog over dry kibble.

This is just one example of many I could give of this phenomenon, which I call pronoun muteness. I have told her about it, but she still doesn't understand.

What Kathy thinks is not that she has pronoun muteness but that I have pronoun deafness. If I wanted to hear her, she says, I would.

"That's nice," she said. "...move the laundry from the washer to the drier?"

"What?"

"Would you move the laundry to the drier, since you're up?"

Now I know she hadn't said "you", meaning me, until I asked.

I said, "See. That's one right there. The pronoun thing."

Kathy paused for a slow breath. "I," she said pointing to herself, "don't know what you," she said pointing to me, "are talking about."

I pursed my lips.

"Listen, if you just assume you should do it," she said, "we won't have this problem."

"Right," I said. "That's the best thing. The laundry isn't going to change itself, is it?"

"That's right," she said. "Thank you, honey."

"No, sweetie," I replied. "Thank *you*."

The Game

Kathy has a game she likes to play in bed.

No, not *that*. Her favorite game, once I get into bed, is to see if she can get me back out of it.

We follow a routine when we turn in for the night. I take the dog out for one last walk, Kathy feeds the cats, I turn down the bed, and Kathy washes her face and does whatever mysterious things a woman does in the bathroom at the end of the day. Most nights, by the time I get to the bed Kathy is already there.

"Ahhhh, long day," I say as I climb in. The sheets are smooth and cool, and the bed is flat and soft. Even the ceiling is soothing. My eyes drift closed. Ahhhh, the silence, it's so good.

"Are the doors locked?"

My eyes open again. "What?"

Kathy turns her mouth to my ear. "Are the doors locked?"

"Yep."

"Are you sure?"

I'm pretty sure, but less sure now that I have to think about it. "Yep," I say.

"They weren't locked yesterday."

This is true. Kathy noticed I forgot to lock the doors after I brought the dog back in. She walked to the door and turned the lock while looking at me. No words were spoken, although she did raise a single eyebrow.

When Kathy reminds me the doors were not locked yesterday she is really pointing out that I am prone to forget things, which I am, and that our safety depends on locking the door, which it does, and that locking it is my responsibility, which it is. Her one little statement is an invocation to the God of Fairness to place the Crown of Responsibility upon my head.

You might ask, why didn't she check today like she did yesterday? Because she didn't. And why doesn't that matter? The answer is this: because I am the forgetter in our marriage and Kathy is not. How did this assessment come to be? That's simple. I keep forgetting things and Kathy doesn't. But it's more than that. Time has shown me to be absent minded and the experience has hardened into a fact that transcends other more recent and transient evidence. I forget. She does not. Put it on our gravestones side by side: FORGETS and NEVER FORGETS.

Kathy did not forget to check the doors tonight because she *does not* forget, and I did forget (maybe) because I *do* forget.

I explain all this to show that while the conversation looks simple, it is complex beneath the surface.

"True," I answer. I forgot to lock the door yesterday. I am acknowledging her citation of my forgetfulness while denying its applicability in this particular case.

Kathy is having none of it. She drums her fingers on my arm. Finger drumming is a recognized signal between us that broadly means "You are testing my patience." In this case she is telling me that her reference to my forgetfulness *is* germane and that we could both save a lot of argument if I would get out of bed and check the lock.

I'm caught. Unless I can specifically recall locking the door I will not get the benefit of the doubt. What can I do? Was I going to put my comfort ahead of our safety? Of course not.

I said, "Rrrrr," and got out of bed. This exact scene has happened many times. Sometimes the door is locked and sometimes it isn't. I don't remember which it was that night, and it doesn't matter.

What matters is that Kathy scored a get-out-of-bed point on me. Kathy 1, Charlie 0.

The locked door is Kathy's favorite ploy, but there are others. Any time a cat yowls, or something makes a banging noise, or Kathy needs an aspirin, I have to get out of bed. Why me? Because it's my job. Things that go bang at night could be dangerous, and if it could be dangerous it's my job to check it out.

Any time I get in the bed and Kathy is able to get me back out of it, she scores. Any time I remain in bed, I score.

Picture this: a film montage of me getting into bed followed by me getting out of bed. In, out, in out. Kathy remains in bed throughout. That's what my life looks like played at fast speed.

I have gotten Kathy out of bed only one time that I can remember. There may have been other times, but if there were I have forgotten them. That particular night I made it to the bed first because I had a cold and was not feeling well.

Kathy climbed in. Ahhh.

I sniffled hard. I felt awful.

"You sound terrible," said Kathy. "You should get some aspirin." She was implying that I should get out of bed to get it.

I sank deeper into the sheets. I was so miserable. "Could you do it?"

"Rrrrr," she said. She got out of bed and brought me the medicine, and I felt much better.

But victories like these are few and only fodder for new losses. A couple of days later something else happened, whatever it was, and Kathy wanted me to get out of bed.

"Maybe you should do it," I said.

"I did it last time," she said.

"What?"

"I got you that aspirin."
"Ah," I said.
Kathy drummed her fingers.

Battles

Marriage, it seems to me, is a game of give and take. Give a little here to take a little there. Overlook your partner's faults so they will give you a break on yours. No one is perfect and everyone needs a little mercy.

Not that you can always stand by quietly and ignore real problems that come up. When you have to take a stand, you have to take a stand. The art of staying married consists of knowing when to stand your ground and when to yield. It takes wisdom, patience, and love. Every day, I firmly believe, should start with a quiet utterance of the Serenity Prayer by husband and wife.

The other day Kathy and I sat down to morning coffee, a ritual we practice every weekend morning. We use the time to start our day, talk over kitchen table issues, and generally connect with each other before the to and fro of life sweeps us along.

That particular morning we discussed Kathy's plans to paint ceramic figurines for Christmas presents and the details of going back to Washington State to visit family.

Oh, and one other thing.

Kathy and I sat at our dining room table, sipping our coffee. It was a warm day in August so I went without socks. When I crossed one leg over the other, my right foot dangled where she could see it.

She looked over the rim of her coffee cup at the foot, then back up at me. "When are you going to cut those nasty toenails? They're looking gross."

I felt like I had been slapped. Here we were, having morning coffee and she had to bring up my feet! Did she have to notice every detail every day? Couldn't she ever let anything go? It got a little old to feel like I was under constant surveillance, including the length of my toenails. Give me a break!

I summed up these thoughts in a single sentence, spoken one syllable at a time so that she would be sure to hear it clearly.

I said, "Pick your battles."

I held Kathy's gaze for a moment and she mine. She knew she had just gotten on my nerves. We understood each other.

"Okay..." she said, continuing to hold my gaze. She too spoke to be heard. "...Cut those nasty toenails."

And the next moment we both started laughing. "Well played," I said.

"You think so?"

"Absolutely."

Balance

Kathy came home from work with her jaw clenched. I was there when she walked through the front door. "What's the matter, sweetie?" I said.

She reached into her pocket and slapped a twenty dollar bill on the countertop. "Stupid damn bonus!"

"You got a bonus? What's wrong with that?" I moved in to give Kathy a big hug, but I also looked over her shoulder at the twenty. It looked okay to me.

"Never mind," she said.

"Sweetie, what's the matter." I hugged her gently. "Tell me."

"No."

"Please...?" I rubbed her back and hugged her a little more.

I felt her shoulder muscles loosen just a bit. "Okay, fine," she said, and she told me.

Kathy has a part time job doing administrative work at a wholesaler. Another administrator who has worked there for years has been training her. Kathy has been learning the job quickly but she had never had to do it all by herself.

Until today. It was Kathy's day off and she was at home when the phone rang. It was Steve, her manager. The other administrator was sick and couldn't come into work today and there were $10,000 worth of sales that needed to be processed and deposited in the bank. Could she come in and take care of it?

Kathy agreed. She finished off what she had been doing at home and went off to work.

It went very well. She did all the bookkeeping for the sales, counted up the money in the cash register, and put together a deposit. Everything balanced to the penny. Not bad for a first try.

Steve came by at the end of the day, and when Kathy told him that the deposit was completely in balance and ready to go, he was impressed.

He said, "Thank you so much for coming in today. That really, really helped."

"You're welcome," said Kathy.

"No really," said Steve, "you were great. So, tell you what..." Steve walked up to the cash register. He struck it with the side of his fist and the drawer flew open. He pulled out a twenty dollar bill and slammed the drawer shut. The bell on the register went *ding*.

"But..." said Kathy.

"Here you go," said Steve, holding out the twenty to her.

"But I just balanced that drawer!"

"I know. Thanks." He waggled the twenty in front of her.

"Now the drawer is twenty dollars short. It's not balanced."

"What?" Steve paused, thinking. "Oh! Well, yeah, I guess. But the point is that you did balance it, so I want to thank you."

"But..."

"Here you go." Steve set the twenty on the desk in front of her. "Take it. Buy a nice dinner. Or buy a present for your husband. Whatever you want. All I want to say is, thank you."

Kathy could see that Steve wasn't going to take no for an answer, so she put the twenty in her pocket. "Thanks," she said.

"You bet," said Steve and he went back to his office.

Kathy thought about sneaking the twenty back into the drawer, but was afraid she would get caught if the drawer suddenly balanced again, so she gave up. She left the money in her pocket, and at the end of the day she came home.

"I'm sorry, sweetie." I was still hugging Kathy. "He just didn't get it, did he?"

"No. I worked really hard to make it all perfect, and..."

"I know, babe, I know. So, um, what kind of present were you going to get me?"

Kathy pulled back. "Well," she said, "I was thinking of gold plating my foot and kicking you in the ass. How does that sound?"

"Twenty-four carat gold?"

Kathy snorted. "For you? Fourteen."

"Nope," I said. "Got to be at least eighteen. I have standards."

"Twenty dollars doesn't buy much eighteen carat gold. I could only do my big toe."

"If it's your big toe, it's good enough for me."

"Oh, honey!"

And we hugged some more.

Feelin' the Love

My love for Kathy burns with an eternal flame. This summer we will have known each other for ten years and celebrate our seventh wedding anniversary. We have long since passed the time in our relationship where it is based on flowers and candy, yet it still goes strong, 'til death do us part.

But it isn't always obvious. To less experienced couples the past few days would have seemed less than passionate, and yet they would have been wrong.

Two weeks ago Kathy fell into a patch of bad mood. This happens periodically, times when Kathy is not her usual chirpy self. It doesn't bother me: into every life some rain must fall. She does not like to talk at times like these, but she does like to cuddle with me on the couch and watch old movies. She lets me hold her and feed her French fries and milk chocolate.

Even when Kathy's bad mood passed after a couple of days, there was still more rain to fall. I came down with a cold that put me on my back for a week. I swallowed buckets of sinus drainage down my sore throat and tried to stay warm. I coughed a lot, especially at night. Kathy did not complain, although she did roll over to turn her back to me. Full kisses were harder to get too, not that I could blame her. Women don't like to kiss men with weepy eyes.

She did other things for me to make up for the missing kisses. When the snow fell hard she went out to shovel it by herself. Normally I would shovel too, but she went out alone without complaint so I could rest.

I recovered to almost full strength later in the week. I started to feel perky, and when I sniffed almost nothing sucked in.

But life was not quite yet back to normal. That morning Kathy shuffled slowly out of the bedroom, stooped half over.

"What's the matter, sweetie?" I asked.

"Back," she said.

I took a step backward. "What's the matter, sweetie?"

Kathy stopped shuffling and turned to look at me. "Back. My back is killing me." She winced. Lower back pain slows Kathy down every now and then.

She grimaced as she bent over to pick up a cat toy, then shuffled over to the next one.

I quickstepped over to her. "Let me get those."

She looked up and winced. "...Okay."

Kathy spent most of the week on the couch: it takes days to recover from lower back pain. She let me rub sports cream on her back each morning and each night before going to bed. I worked at the knots in her muscles until they burned with icy heat and the sting of menthol wafted upward from her white skin into my nose.

Kathy's health eventually improved. Her stance returned to its normal upright position, and when she got up this morning I patted her back. "Morning, sweetie!"

"Ooh - careful! I'm still sore."

"Sorry, baby," I said. But I knew she wouldn't be sore much longer.

"Love you!" she said, leaning her head painfully onto my shoulder.

"Love you too!" I said. I rubbed my nose with my hand and stroked her hair.

That's right. Love, still going strong.

My Darling Husband

I try to be a thoughtful husband. I really try. And yet, despite the fact that I've been married to Kathy for seven years, there are some things I still mess up over and over.

I could talk about how every time I wash my hands I cover the entire counter with water, or how I have never, ever cooked a meal, or how the covers always end up on my side of the bed, where, by the way, all the snoring comes from. The list of my shortcomings is long and I could talk about any of them, but it's February, almost Valentine's Day, so I want to talk about gifts and greeting cards.

Kathy loves gifts and she uses any holiday as an excuse to give and receive them. Before I got married the two gift-giving holidays were Christmas and birthdays. That was all we had when I was growing up, and it was all we needed.

The rules changed after I got married. You can imagine my feeling of uncertainty when, in our first year together, Kathy asked me what I wanted for Valentine's Day. It had never occurred to me that I should get a gift. Maybe flowers and candy, but not presents. The idea was completely new to me, and frightening.

Of course I understood that her asking me what I wanted contained an implied message, that she wanted a gift too. How was I supposed to know what she wanted? I've never been someone who could buy things for other people that they didn't expect but fell in love with. I didn't like this change at all. I had had enough trouble buying Christmas presents for

Kathy, and it seemed unfair to have another gift giving holiday so soon.

But I tried. I went to the mall and wandered heavy-footed up and down the stores, past the perfume she wears, past the leather purse she had her eye on, and past the books she wanted to read. Please, God, tell me what she would like so I can get out of this mall!

I was almost ready to give up when I drifted into Brookstone, a store that sells useful and imaginative items to urban professionals. Most of their products are digital in some way, or are made from glossy plastic or stainless steel. They are trendy and elegant, and priced accordingly. They were just the kind of things, I was sure, Kathy would like.

I didn't buy the digital pedometer with the heart rate meter, and I didn't buy the brushed steel shower curtain rod, and I didn't buy the machine that plays ocean sounds - Atlantic *and* Pacific - to help you fall asleep, although all of those would have made excellent gifts. No, I bought a U-shaped pillow for her neck made from the most scientifically advanced foam rubber ever created. Her neck bothers her most of the time and I thought she would appreciate a pillow to help with it.

I still remember Kathy's face when she pulled the pillow out of the paper sack I had wrapped it in. Her fingers dug into its soft sponginess, testing it, enjoying it already. I imagined the horseshoe shaped pillow looked like a smile.

"Happy Valentine's Day, baby," I cooed. "I love you."

Kathy squeezed the pillow again, hard. "What is it?"

"It's a pillow for your neck. You wear it to bed like a collar and it's supposed to help with your neck pain." I wrapped my hands around my neck to demonstrate the collar effect.

She blinked. "Thanks," she said. "I'll wear it tonight," and she put it on the coffee table.

"Awesome," I said, "and I'll try the clothes you got for me." I had never worn a satin leopard-print G-string before, but I was willing to try it.

We went to bed that night and she tucked her head into the gap in the foam pillow.

Then I said something I shouldn't have said. I whispered in her ear, "I hope it helps, sweetie, because that pillow cost eighty dollars."

Kathy sat straight up in bed. She clapped her hands twice and the bedroom light came on. "What! You paid eighty dollars for this?"

"Well," I said, starting to feel defensive, "yes."

"It's just a piece of foam rubber. Where on earth do you go to buy an eighty dollar piece of foam rubber?"

"Hey, that's not nice!" I said. "I was thinking about your sore neck!"

"Very romantic, Romeo. This is a stupid gift, even for you." She picked the pillow off the bed and threw it to the floor. "You can take it back tomorrow and get our money back."

Now I was really mad. "Fine!" I said. "You can take this stupid G-string back. It's not very comfortable!" I reached down below the covers and fought to take it off, which was not easy to do lying on my back. I pulled it out from under the covers and threw it in her face. "Take it. I'd rather be naked than wear it."

"Fine," said Kathy. She pinched the G-String off her face and tossed it next to the pillow, then clapped twice again and the lights went back out. She rolled onto her side away from me and tried to go to sleep, and I did the same, satisfied that I would have the last laugh when I snored all night and took all the covers.

I said I was going to talk about greeting cards, so why haven't I said anything about them yet? Because I didn't start to buy them until after the disastrous Valentine's Day I just described. From that day on I was not asked to buy any more presents on my own, and we established a system where she tells me what she wants, then she buys it, and we both pretend it's from me. Everyone is happy: I don't have to shop and she gets what she likes.

The only thing I am still responsible for is the greeting card. She buys her own presents and I buy her a card. That's the deal. Simple, right?

Yes, it's so simple a moron could do it, and yet I still struggle with it.

I struggle with forgetfulness every holiday. I know I have to buy a card, and I have plenty of time. I have two months, then six weeks, then one month, then - BAM! - twelve hours. The last three weeks fly at me like a windshield flies at a bug.

I've gotten caught by surprise and screwed up more than once. It's embarrassing but true.

Take the year I got Kathy two wedding anniversary cards for her birthday. That's not as big a mistake as you might think. It so happens our anniversary and her birthday are one day apart. That means she gets presents for both days, and it means I need to buy her two cards.

I forgot the cards until the last minute. Thankfully I live near a Rite Aid and I was able to lie to Kathy and say I needed to get gas for the car when what I really needed to do was buy cards.

I made quick work at the Rite Aid. I was in a hurry and I must not have looked at the cards carefully when I bought them. That would explain why, after we all sang Happy Birthday and she blew out the candles on her cake and opened the card from me, it said, "I'm So Glad I Married You, My Darling Bride".

Kathy set the card down and looked up at me. She tried to catch my eye and hold it, but I wouldn't let her. I stared down at the cake and watched the smoke coming off the extinguished candles.

"Where's my birthday card?" she asked.

"I love you, punkin'," I said.

"Did you get me a birthday card?"

"Of course I did," I said. "Hey, you ready to have some cake?"

Kathy considered what to say and must have decided there was no point in asking me any more questions. "Cake? Sure! I guess I'll see my birthday card tomorrow!" We all laughed and ate some very delicious birthday cake.

She was wrong about the other card. I gave it to her the next evening, on our anniversary, and it wasn't a birthday card. It was another anniversary card. This one said, "To My Wonderful Husband on Our Special Day Together". It was covered with white roses and there were two champagne glasses sparkling under candlelight. It was so lovely I could hardly believe I had picked it out myself. I would have loved to receive a card like this one.

Kathy said, "It's not a birthday card, is it?"

"Um, no."

"And it's not a card for a wife."

Was that a question? I wasn't sure. "Um, no," I said just to be safe.

"Well. Happy birthday to me."

"That's right," I said. "And happy anniversary. Give me a hug."

Kathy deserved better. I promised myself I would pay closer attention to the calendar, and always get her cards on time, and make sure they were for the right event.

And I mostly succeeded for a few years.

That is, until we took a trip to my mother's house on February 12th. Her house was five hundred miles away at the time, an all day drive. The morning of the 14th, just before we were set to come home, Kathy gave me my Valentine's Day card and a box of chocolates. She had remembered the holiday and the fact that she wouldn't be home, and had bought the card in advance. She had thought ahead and was prepared.

What about me? I was empty handed. I had not taken the trip into account and thought I was going to have two more days to get a card, so I hadn't gotten her one. I asked myself the whole drive home how I had made such a stupid mistake.

I tried to make it up to her the next day, better late than never. I told Kathy I was going out to gas up the car.

"Great," she said. "Could you buy a box of chocolates? I want to get something for Maryam. Maryam was a neighbor friend who had watched our home while we were gone.

"Sure," I said.

"And..." she said, "we're almost out of condoms."

I said, "Oh reeealllly?"

"Forget it - I've got to clean the house today. It's a pig sty."

"Oh, okay." I should have known better. The day after coming home from a trip is always house cleaning day. I wanted to rip the dustrag out of her hand and coat her face with kisses, but the look in her eyes said no.

Let me tell you, there aren't many cards left at Rite Aid after Valentine's Day. I can still see the thin dabbling of red, white, and pink on all those blue shelves. The quality was poor too. No more white roses or champagne glasses. No more Anne Geddes babies in heart shaped bassinets. No more soft focus couples holding hands on a beach at sunset. The choices were these: Elmer Fudd as Cupid with his bow and arrow, red bowling balls in the shape of a heart, or Dilbert offering a bouquet of roses to Dogbert.

My stomach tightened when I saw what I would have to bring home to Kathy, and I swore I would never, never mess up like this again.

Which one did I pick? I don't want to say. I just don't, okay?

I made a choice and the hard job was done. I went to pick up a box of condoms and a box of candy for Maryam, and I walked to the checkout line. I set my things down on the counter in front of a middle-aged woman wearing a blue vest and a name tag.

It was at this point that I realized the things I was buying might seem to tell a story to the clerk. It was the story of a loser who comes into a drug store the day after Valentine's Day, buys a card and a seven dollar box of chocolates, and who thinks he's so hot he still might get lucky.

And, I asked myself, even though the chocolates weren't for Kathy, would the clerk have been so wrong?

The clerk made no comment on my purchase, but when I looked at her name tag it said this:

Hi! My name is **DORIS**
You make me sick!

That was the worst for awhile. More holidays passed and I mostly remembered to get cards on time.

I did not fail again until last Christmas.

Kathy had already bought all the Christmas presents for family, for friends, for herself, and for me. All I had to do was get a card and some candy so that she could open them with presents on the night of Christmas Eve.

Flash forward to 1:32 PM on Christmas Eve. "Sweetie," I said, "I'm going to gas up the car."

At 1:40 I was standing in Rite Aid in front of the Christmas cards. It wasn't the Rite Aid where I had met Doris, but I still had the same problem.

I was not the only one looking at cards. There were two other women there who I'm sure were shopping for Christmas cards for next year. I didn't want to get in their way, so I picked a card quickly. Maybe too quickly.

Kathy, her sister Marti, and I opened presents in the living room later that night. Soft snow covered the ground outside. Nat King Cole sang Christmas songs on the stereo, and the lights from the Christmas tree cast moving shadows on our faces.

When it was my turn to open the card from Kathy, it said this:

To My Darling Husband on This Christmas Day

Many are the thoughts I've had of you, my Husband, my Love
And of the Life we have built together
The Joys
And the Sorrows.
Our bonds of Love continue
To Grow and Grow
And There is no one I would rather Share all my Days with
Than You,
My Darling Husband
My Love

(signed)
I Love You Always,
~~~Kathy~~~
OOO XXX OOO

What can I say? I was touched. Kathy and I have built a life together and it brings us both great comfort and joy.

Then Kathy opened her card from me, the one I had bought earlier that day, and it read like this:

Seasons Greetings!
(signed)
Merry Christmas,
Charlie
XXX

Kathy didn't say anything. She handed the card to Marti, who opened it and read it twice.

"Season's Greetings?" she said.

"Um," I answered.

"Season's Greetings?"

I crossed my arms over my chest. "Hellooo?? It's a Christmas card."

"It's a lame card," said Marti. "That's what it is." She threw it down on the coffee table.

What could I say? It was a lame card.

Now Kathy's arms were crossed over her chest. "Yeah - lame."

She looked at me, and I at her. She uncrossed her arms and looked away, and she tried to act like she was just annoyed with my careless gift, but I saw then that she wasn't just annoyed.

I said earlier the list of my shortcomings is long, and it's more than that. My list of this one shortcoming - forgetting things for Kathy - is also long. The only thing I have working in my favor is that there is always another holiday and another chance. I used to dread Valentine's Day, or resent it for the presents I had to buy, but now I am grateful for it because it gives me another chance to make up for the mistakes I make at Christmas.

Captain Pants

This is the story of how I replaced a $120 pair of dress shoes with a $25 pair.

I have almost completely worn out the pair of leather dress shoes that I wear to work every day. I need a new pair and winter is coming. I like the shoes and would otherwise go back to the same store and buy another pair, but I can't. I can't because I bought them at Well-Dressed Man, and I can't go back there, not now.

Well-Dressed Man, in case you don't know, is a chain of clothing stores specializing in men's business attire. They are very good at what they do and I have been a customer for years.

In fact, they are so good at what they do that I have to be careful about going there. Well-Dressed Man is strong medicine, powerful stuff. Every time I walk into one of their stores, I must be prepared to give them at least five hundred dollars.

There is no protection from this fact and there are no exceptions. Let me describe a typical visit so that you may see it for yourself.

I said to Kathy the last time we went, "I need a new pair of pants."

Kathy agreed and we went the following Saturday. The sun was shining that day. It was spring and the birds were coming back into the trees and singing love songs to other birds. Life was good, I thought, as Kathy and I walked hand-in-hand through the front door of Well-Dressed Man to buy a pair of dress pants.

The tone inside the store was calm, appropriate for buying a business suit, yet still friendly and bustling with the talk of men and the staff trying to help them. Calm and energetic, you see, calm and energetic.

A fashion associate noticed us immediately and asked us if we were looking for anything in particular. We told him we were looking for a pair of pants, and he led us to a long rack of them and stepped away to let us browse.

Well, you know how it goes. One pair of pants turned into two pair, then three, and then Kathy started to think of other things I might need pants for.

"What if," Kathy asked, "you have to visit a Navy captain on a submarine? You'll want to have some dark blue pants with a stripe down the leg." She held up just such a pair. "They have them in your size."

How could I argue with that? Would I want to look bad in front of the captain? I don't think so! Yet it doesn't take many of these imaginary precautions to add up to real money.

And this was before the sales associate had said anything. He didn't need to because he had the power of the secret heart of Well-Dressed Man on his side: the dressing room. The Dressing Room is the place where a man discovers that the only way to fix his sorry life is to buy more clothes. Different men may reach this conclusion in different ways, but that's where they all end up.

I usually dress casually when I go to Well-Dressed Man. Why wouldn't I? It's Saturday, and I always wear shorts, a T-shirt, and tennis shoes at home. Why wouldn't I wear them shopping?

This makes complete sense until I walk into the dressing room. Then it's just me, the pants, and my mother waiting outside to see how I look in them.

Did I say mother? I meant wife. Kathy is my wife. Sorry.

Anyway, I took off my shorts, which I suddenly realized were two years old and the same style I wore in college, and my shoes, which used to be white but now looked like an old man's teeth, and put on a pair of pants. I pulled them up and put my shoes back on, and began to feel very clearly that I was about to step out onto a sales floor in front of dozens of people and my mother wearing dress pants with ratty shoes, a T-shirt full of holes, and a "never had a real job, what answer did you get for Question Seven, Van Halen is my favorite band but Def Leppard is good too" pair of shorts hanging on a hook behind me.

I asked myself, What do I need to buy to make this sense of insecurity stop? Just tell me. Captain pants? Fine.

Did I notice there was a whole store of men and their wives all doing the same thing, some in their twenties, thirties, forties, fifties, and sixties? No I did not, and even if I had I wouldn't have cared.

I've tried it the other way, too. Sometimes I've worn dress clothes to Well-Dressed Man in order to present myself in the dressing room as a professional who had reached a certain stage in his life and career, as if to say, I may enjoy Van Halen, but I'll never tell. You should assume from the way my belt matches my shoes that I prefer Bach.

The only problem with this approach was that all the clothes I was wearing to symbolize my mature dignity came from Well-Dressed Man, and the sales associate knew it.

"Ah, *Pantalons de Mer*," said the associate, referring to the maker of the pants I was wearing, and eyeing the stripe on the leg. "Those are very popular. Let me show you where we keep them."

The only advantage I have, now that I have reached a certain age, is Kathy. She has an eye for fashion and she understands what kind of clothing is suitable for a man of my station. Best of all, she waits outside the dressing room while I'm changing. Girlfriends don't do this, but wives do, and if there is any better reason to get married than to have someone to hold your hand in a clothing store, I don't know what it is.

Thus far the sales person had done very little. He just led us to the clothes and stepped away. Now he came back and we gave him the pants to ring up, and he said, "These are very nice. Would you like to see some ties to go with these pants?"

Well, I hadn't thought about that. I already had some ties at home, but now I wasn't sure if they would go with the particular blue, green, or tan of these pants. "Um, sure," I said.

And that's how I bought two ties.

That's also how I bought the shirt, three pairs of socks, a belt, and a pair of cedar shoe inserts to make them smell good and hold their shape. How could I have not known I needed these things? And, I must say, I was going to look pretty good in them. Sure, I spent a little more money than I expected to, but that's the price of being well-dressed, and when Kathy and I left the store with a bag of clothes, the sun was still shining and the birds were, if anything, singing a little more brightly.

And now, here I am. The shoes I bought that day are worn out and I need to replace them. I would love to go back to Well-Dressed Man to get a new pair because I really like the shoes. There are only two problems, however. First, I know that the $120 pair of shoes is actually going to cost at least $500. I will walk in with bare feet and walk out decorated like a Christmas tree. It happens every time, and I accept it. That by itself isn't such a big problem because my clothes are getting threadbare and it's time to go shopping anyway.

The other problem is this. How do I say it? Well. Well, it's like this: I have gained a little bit of weight since the last time I went clothes shopping. And I'd like to get back to my normal weight before buying new clothes, because it's like I'd be "locking in" the fatness if I bought new clothes to fit it. Which wouldn't make sense anyway because the extra weight is completely temporary. So my plan is this: lose ten pounds, then go clothes shopping with a clear conscience. That way I have an incentive to keep the weight off because I wouldn't want to waste money on clothes that suddenly don't fit anymore.

That's the plan. Now, as you know, it takes time to lose

weight naturally through proper diet and exercise, and even longer if it's the holiday season, which it happens to be now. If it takes eight months to lose ten pounds, that's okay, because it's more important to do it right than to do it fast.

Unfortunately, I've already worn holes through the bottoms of my $120 Well-Dressed Man dress shoes and I can't go anywhere near a Well-Dressed Man until Mother Nature has returned me to my proper weight and the stores run out of egg nog and frosted Christmas cookies.

I know there are solutions to every problem. For example, I could walk on the edges of my shoes instead of the soles. My ankles might hurt at first, but I could get used to it. Alternatively, I could stand outside Well-Dressed Man and look for a man with size thirteen feet walking in and give him five hundred dollars to bring me back a pair of shoes.

I might also send Kathy into Well-Dressed Man, thinking that, not being a man, she would be immune to spending money there, except that on one visit we discovered they sell leather jackets for women. That was the day we spent a thousand dollars, an experience we can't repeat just to get some shoes.

As you can see, this is not an easy problem to solve, and it will take awhile. In the meantime, I went to a discount shoe store and bought a temporary pair of shoes for $25. They're pretty good, especially for so little money, and if they wear out faster that's okay. They only have to last a few more months.

Rush at the DTE

Rush, my favorite band ever, played a great concert last month at the DTE Energy Music Theatre on a tour dedicated to the 30th anniversary of their first album, released in 1974.

Before I go any further, for those of you have never heard of Rush, here is a primer. Rush is a rock music trio from Toronto whose style does not fit squarely into any genre, but it has been called heavy metal by people who focus on their guitar-heavy sound, progressive rock by people who tune into the virtuosity of the musicians and the intellectual bent of the lyrics, and power pop by people who like their catchy melodies and harmonies.

I don't completely agree with any of these assessments since none of them do justice to the band, which I think is much richer and more interesting than these categories. I, like many others before me, could write a long essay full of opinions and theories about Rush – but not today.

Rush's music appeals most strongly to white boys who like science and math, and is not known for drawing a female audience. It's not a good idea to play Rush for a young lady on a first date, and the list of Rush fans who lost the chance to make out because they didn't understand this, and wanted to share their love for Rush, is long and tragic. Very tragic.

Rush fans might not be the most popular kids in school or have the best social skills, but they are rabid. Rush fans are as loyal as it gets.

I am one of those fans. I discovered Rush as a teenager over twenty years ago and have followed their career ever since.

That is why, when Kathy's sister Marti told me that Rush was coming to town, I immediately bought two tickets over the Internet, one for me and one for Kathy. The power chords of "Tom Sawyer" played in my head as I clicked the mouse and keyboard.

Dum-dum-dum-*CLICKKKKKKKKK*
Dum-dum-dum-*ENTERRRRRRRRR*

I know Marti and Kathy love me because Marti told me about the show and Kathy agreed to go even though they don't like Rush. I've tried for years to explain why they're wrong, but I haven't changed their minds, a classic case of having all the facts on your side and still losing the argument.

I have gone to see Rush almost every time they have come to town. I first went in 1986 when they toured for their *Power Windows* album. They played in Seattle, where I went to college.

I missed a chance to see them a couple years before that when they came to Seattle and I was still living in Spokane. I bit my lip hard, stunned that they should come so close and yet be so far away. I had only just gotten my driver's license and didn't have the gumption to ask to drive 300 miles by myself to see a concert.

I mentioned the show in passing to my mom a few weeks later and she said, "Really? You should have said something. You could have gone."

I was shocked. I thought it wasn't possible to ask for so much. But maybe it wasn't so much after all. My parents knew Rush was important to me. How did they know? Well, it might have been the way I played *Moving Pictures* every day for months when I first discovered it. That record opened up worlds for me. It was *so* heavy, yet *so* skillful, and *so* smart. I had never heard anything so loud and pretty and good. I just...could...not get enough of it.

Maybe it was the fact that I also bought their other eight records as fast as I could save my allowance.

If I had to guess, however, how my parents knew about my obsession with Rush, I would say it was the air drumming.

Of all the things about the band that grabbed me, the thing that grabbed me hardest was Neil Peart's drumming. Up until that time all the drummers I had heard played as if their job was just to keep time and to stay in the background. Ringo Starr is a good example of this style. He played well and did not draw any attention to himself.

Peart was different. He was a fully equal member of the band, and the more I listened to his playing, the more I heard in it. Going into the first chorus he might play a simple fill, but going into the second chorus he would play a more complex fill. He kept time with the ride cymbal, then with quarter notes on the hi-hat cymbals, then with sixteenth notes. Everything he did commented on what the other players were doing, all the time. Even if I turned off the bass, guitar, and vocals, a Rush song would still sound energetic and compelling just because of the drums.

I have always loved drumming and this was the most intense and innovative drumming I had ever heard up to that time. I buzzed right into it and stuck like a fly on honey.

Even better, Peart wrote the lyrics to all the songs, which were fascinating in their own right. "2112" is a twenty-minute opera about the world of the future, where people live under the dictatorship of the Priests of the Temple of Syrinx. Their tyrannical hold on the people is broken by a boy who discovers a decadent artifact of the past...a guitar.

Another opera, "Hemispheres", tells the story of the war between Dionysus (Heart) and Apollo (Mind) and shows how instead of fighting each other they should live together in harmony.

I was thrilled. The Heart and the Mind *should* live in harmony. Nothing on the radio talked about these things. When I discovered Rush, the radio was filled with New Wave bands like Duran Duran who sang about the same boring subjects -

love, mostly. In those days the last thing I needed was another silly love song. That's why Rush was so important, and Neil Peart in particular.

It wasn't enough for me to listen to the drumming. I had to try to play it too. I did not own a drumset, but I did own a pair of drumsticks. I sat in a chair in the corner of the living room and played Rush records through a pair of chunky white plastic headphones with the volume dial turned way up. In my mind I sat at a drumset, massive like Neil's, and I played it with my sticks in the air. This would have been a hard thing for Mom and Dad not to notice, what with both of them sitting in the living room watching TV.

tick-tick-tick-tick "Tonight on *60 Minutes...*"
...race back to the farm, to dream with my uncle at the fi-re-side...
[-chug chugga-chugga BASH SPLASH CRASH]

I did not get to see Rush play in Seattle that year, but my parents did agree to let me watch their MTV concert. Rush had filmed the show that was also released as the concert album *Exit...Stage Left*. MTV, still young in those days and still trying to scrape a profit out of playing music, aired it as a Saturday Night Concert.

I watched the concert sitting cross-legged directly in front of the television, so close I could have touched the screen with my elbows.

It was great. What can I say? It was great. Nothing more needs to be said. It was really, really great.

My parents chose not to leave the room while I watched the show. Afterward I asked my dad, "So, what did you think?"

"Sounds just like their records," he said.

Tears of joy welled up in my eyes. I couldn't have agreed more.

Those days were the honeymoon of my Rush fandom, when everything they did was new and interesting and important. Only a true fan like me would know that Rush releases a concert album after every fourth studio album, neither more nor less, and only a true fan would notice that the fade-out of "Red Barchetta" includes bass punches - two, then one, then one, then two again: "2112". I could go on, but I think you get the idea.

As high school faded into college and college drifted into my early days in the working world, the relationship cooled and deepened. I developed passionate loves for other bands, and I came to realize that not everything about Rush's music was the best in every way. My musical world broadened and Rush's place in it inevitably seemed to diminish.

But it didn't matter. My bond with Rush was stronger than the transient musical thrills of the moment. After a belated enthusiasm for Duran Duran had waxed and waned (They turned out to be pretty good after all despite the love songs.) Rush was still there. I go through revivals every few years, a span of a few days when I play nothing but Rush. This is my way of reconnecting, something I do with all the bands that have been with me for a long time.

Then I met Kathy in the mid-1990s, after the release of *Counterparts* but before the release of *Test for Echo*.

Kathy does not like Rush or understand them, but despite her dislike she was prepared to live and let live. I could listen to Rush all I wanted as long as I didn't make her listen to it. That was our deal.

Which I broke a couple years later. That spring Rush came to play the Gorge Amphitheater outside the town of George, Washington. The Gorge is 150 miles away from Seattle and Kathy, unlike my mom, was not willing to let me drive that far by myself. I didn't have anyone else to go with so she grudgingly agreed to join me.

Rush was not the only show we went to that spring. We also bought tickets to *Defending the Caveman*, a comic one man show about the differences between the way men and women view the world. Kathy was excited to see it and we both expected to have a fun night.

We saw *Defending the Caveman* first. I pulled the tickets out of the desk drawer and we drove twenty miles to the Moore Theater in downtown Seattle. When we got to the door I pulled out the tickets and saw that I had grabbed the tickets to the Rush concert. The *Caveman* tickets were still at home in the desk.

"Ummm..." I said.

"What?" said Kathy.

"Uh...ummmmm..."

We drove home very fast and Kathy remained silent. I could not have pushed a quarter between her lips, they were pressed together so hard, and when we arrived home, Kathy ran in to get the right tickets and we drove back even faster. We took our seats just in time, and the show, which shone a bright light on the differences between the sexes, was very funny. It was a good thing the show made me laugh because I felt I had already gotten a big dose of *la difference* before the curtain went up.

We went to see Rush a few weeks later. The Gorge is an open-air amphitheater overlooking the Columbia River. It was a warm night in May in central Washington. For most people this part of the state is nothing more than a wide desert between Seattle and Spokane, a place to travel through but not a place to be. It takes nights like that one, with every star visible, to make know-it-all people from Seattle slow down even for a minute.

Kathy and I arrived via a long dirt road. Cardboard signs directed us to park in an enormous grass field where men and women in yellow jackets directed each car into the next open slot. The sun was just starting to set.

We got out of the car and made a mental note of where we were parked, and walked to the amphitheater.

Kathy and I were like drops of rainwater on a window, surrounded by other raindrops all meandering to the bottom, and as we converged on the same place I could see the others more clearly.

My people.

There were the young men, not so different from what I had been, who were tall and still thin and who wore T-shirts promoting more recent albums like *Roll the Bones* and *Hold Your Fire*. They walked by themselves, having an unusually high threshold for introspection and solitude, or they banded together with one or two other young men and seemed to be laughing at jokes no one else could understand.

Then there were the old-timers, men in their forties and fifties with bushy mustaches and wallets attached to their beltloops by lengths of chain. They thought of Rush as a 70s-style guitar-riffing rock and roll band, like Led Zeppelin or Black Sabbath, and they preferred to forget that the band, like almost everyone else, softened their sound in the 1980s and experimented with synthesizers. They wore T-shirts from the early records like *Caress of Steel* and *A Farewell to Kings*. Many of the shirts were faded and had holes where the cotton had worn through. But that was to be expected. It's hard to take care of a T-shirt for twenty years, especially if you wear it every day.

We all came from different generations and musical backgrounds, but tonight it didn't matter. Rush brought us together and allowed us to bridge the gaps.

Kathy, meanwhile, resolved to make the best of it. She had brought a blanket and made a basket of food so that we could be well nourished and so she could pretend that the reason we were here was to have a picnic.

We took our seats on the ground in the bowl of the amphitheater, where we had a good view of the stage. I could see Neil Peart's drumset. It was huge, filled with drums the way a crocodile's mouth is filled with teeth and covered with a mushroom field of brassy cymbals. You couldn't swing a drumstick anywhere and not make music sitting at a kit like that.

I resisted the temptation to get up and walk to the front of the stage for a closer look.

Not so the man behind me.

"Whoa! Check it out!"

I heard him stand up and ankle-walk past the knees of the people next to him. I saw out of the corner of my eye a man wearing parachute pants and a mullet haircut move to the stage with both hands stretched out in front of him.

Kathy and I looked behind us at the space where he had been. There was a woman there (really - a woman!), smiling. "He just loves Neil Peart," she said.

Kathy bit her lip. "Ee-yup," she said. She popped a seedless grape into her mouth.

Then the sun went down. Kathy pulled out her book and a small reading light and I continued to watch the stage for clues.

I waited and balled my fists and tapped my feet until the stage lights went down and the crowd jumped up. The band came out, and they played a great show.

There isn't much to say about it. If you want to know what it sounded like, the tour was captured on *Different Stages*, released after their sixteenth studio album. (The four-album rule still applies!) The band played a mix of old and new, fast and slow. They even played all of "2112", not just the first two movements they usually play.

Like everyone else I stood up for most of the show, clapping and hooting. Everyone, that is, except Kathy. She remained seated and snacked on cheese, summer sausage, and buttery crackers. Once when I looked down I saw her pour ice tea from a thermos into a plastic tumbler to wash down the bite-size cherry tart she had just eaten. She looked up at me and smiled with her lips but not her eyes.

The show ended. The stage lights went dark and left only the streetlights posted here and there among the audience. We picked up our things, all twenty-some thousand of us, and wandered back the way we came. The loudest sounds were the conversations around us that sounded so much more intimate now after three hours of amplified music. I could hear every murmur.

One of those conversations came from behind. The man in the parachute pants was speaking to his date. He quoted from the lyrics of "The Spirit of Radio" slowly and with emphasis, as if they were scripture.

All this machinery
Making modern music
Can still be open-hearted
Not so coldly charted
It's really just a question
Of your honesty
Yeah   your   honesty

I gave up being fifteen a long time ago. I take things much less seriously than I used to, so when I heard Parachute Pants I laughed to myself and thought, "Lighten up, buddy." But still, I'd be lying if I didn't admit that, just a little bit, I thought, "Yeah, your honesty – *yeah.*"

We passed en masse out of the amphitheater through the narrow exits. That was the moment where all of us turned back into each of us.

"Did you have a good time, honey?" Kathy asked.

"Yep. Sure did. How about you?"

"Ha!"

We wandered out to the field where the cars were parked. The night had turned cool. The people, who had exited the amphitheater almost solemnly, regained themselves and began to whoop and call out to each other. The tone picked up in spirit until it sounded more like a giant tailgate party.

Cars pulled out and began to form long lines that nudged through the crowds of people. Kathy and I were still among the walkers.

Here's the thing to understand that we learned the hard way. The parking field at the Gorge is huge, really huge, and even though we parked in the daylight, it was dark when we had to find our car. Even if we had done a better job of taking note of landmarks to remember where we had parked, it would not have helped because the landmarks were no longer visible and every car had turned to black. Our car, which had started out the night colored green and located right where we had left it, was now somewhere - somewhere! - in that field.

Kathy and I drifted up and down, then side to side, then up and down again. Kathy, who had not wanted to come in the first place, did not appreciate having to wander around in a field just to get home, and I didn't like it either. Marital harmony, usually so strong between us, began to break down.

"Charlie, I want to find the damn car! Where did you put it?"

"I don't *know*. If I *did* we'd be *there* now, *okay?*"

"I can't believe I came to this. I could be at home right now taking a bubble bath instead of listening for four hours to a singer who sounds like a little girl! *Ooooh Tom Sawyer Ahhhh-ahh-ahhhhhh!*"

"Shut up! Geddy Lee does not sound like Katherine Hepburn."

"Oh yes he does."

"I think the car is that way," I said.

"No it isn't. We already went that way." She pointed ahead.

"No, we already went that way." I pointed back and to the left.

"Nooo, you're thinking about the yellow chick-magnet van we passed twenty minutes ago. It was over there, not over there."

"Oh."

All of this was in the first half hour of searching. Altogether we searched for ninety minutes. I am not kidding. We looked for our car for almost as long as we watched the concert.

Near the end Kathy, whose attitude did not improve and whose comments about Rush turned increasingly hostile, slumped cross-legged onto the ground. "I'm not doing this anymore. I need to rest."

"Fine," I said and sat down with her.

"Would you like a slice of French bread with some cheese on it?" she asked.

"Sure."

The meal did us good. We calmed down a little and tried to think through what we should do next.

As I ate I pulled my keys out of my pocket and played with them. I noticed that the key fob had a red ALARM button on it. It was supposed to scare off would-be car thieves. Just for laughs I pushed the button.

Honk honk honk honk honk.

"That's our car!" I said. Oh joy! It was only about a hundred feet from where we sat.

"Wooo-hoo!" she yelped. "I told you it was over that way somewhere."

We high-fived, picked up our food and found our car. At last we were able to join the line of people trying to exit.

The next time Rush came to the Gorge I invited my brother Harlan instead of Kathy. All of us were happier for it, and this time I was better prepared for the parking situation. I tied a bright T-shirt on the car antenna and it took only thirty minutes to find the car after the show. One little victory, so to speak.

Which brings us to the present. I live in Michigan now so we won't be going to any more concerts at the Gorge, but that's okay. Rush came to Detroit a few days ago.

I bought the tickets a month in advance and every day I drove I-75 to work past a giant billboard whose bright lights read:

RUSH
June 8th

I drove past the announcement two or three times a week. The same sign also advertised Britney Spears and Kid Rock, but they did not make me smile the way Rush did.

Then came last week. I thought, "Next Wednesday I'm going to see Rush. Duh-duh-duh-*duhhhhhhh!*"

On Tuesday, June 7th I stayed home and watched Game 2 of the NBA finals between the Los Angeles Lakers and my hometown Detroit Pistons. They played neck-and-neck the whole game and the Lakers would have lost if Kobe Bryant had not made a 3-point shot with two seconds to play in the fourth quarter and gone on to dominate the overtime. You couldn't have asked for a better game.

However, while the basketball game did not end in the fourth quarter, something else did.

With six minutes left to play Kathy, who had been working in the other room, came out and called to me in the living room. "Charlie...I've got bad news."

I got up and we met in the hallway. She looked stricken. "I found the Rush tickets. The show is tonight."

"Oh." It was 10:30. The band was playing at that moment.

"I wanted to make sure we had the tickets so I looked in the desk and they said June 8th and that's today. When you said Wednesday I didn't think anything about it. I'm really sorry."

"Oh," I said.

"I am so sorry."

"Yeah," I said. "It's okay." Somewhere I had convinced myself that June 8th was Wednesday, not Tuesday.

What could I say? I had not paid attention. The show went on without me, and I had no one to blame but myself.

I said earlier that Rush came to the DTE and played a great show. How do I know that? Because they always play a great show. I just happened not to be there.

I didn't feel it much that night, but the next day I was mad. I really hated to miss the show. I really, really hated it.

But in the end concerts come and go, even Rush concerts. I would have loved to see them but I've seen them before, and if they could stay together for thirty years why not go for sixty?

No, what bothered me was that I could miss the show on account of such a stupid mistake. How old and senile and careless am I that I could mix up the date and the day of the week? How much of a fool am I that I did not double check it in time to see my error? What other costly mistakes am I waiting to make? I would never have let this happen when I was fifteen.

So, that's the whole story. All done. I prefer stories to have happier endings than this one. I'm sorry, but I can't oblige this time. I messed up. There is no happy ending.

Still...the mistake reminds me of one other time when I learned a lesson from Rush.

When I was seventeen years old I took the PSAT standardized test. The test is used to measure student performance and influences college admissions. One of the questions on the test stumped me. The answer depended on understanding the meaning of the word "didactical".

I didn't know what it meant, but then I thought of the song "Didacts and Narpets" from *Caress of Steel*. The song lasts for only one minute and has only one intelligible lyric. At the end of the song Geddy Lee screams *"LISTEN!"*

I was able to deduce from that one lyric that "didactical" has something to do with learning or teaching and I was able to guess the answer to the question. I looked the word up after the test and saw that I had answered the question correctly.

Maybe, just maybe, that one correct answer led to a test score that let me get into college (to study math) and cleared the path for everything that has happened since. Not bad for a rock band, eh?

Twenty years later, however, I still don't know what a narpet is.

Credits

race back to the farm... quoted from "Red Barchetta", music by Geddy Lee and Alex Lifeson, lyrics by Neil Peart, lyrics copyright 1981 by CORE Music Publishing.

All this machinery... quoted from "The Spirit of Radio", music by Geddy Lee and Alex Lifeson, lyrics by Neil Peart, lyrics copyright 1980 by CORE Music Publishing.

Visit the Rush website at rush.com.

Valentine's Day Surprise

In the past, I have had trouble with buying cards and gifts for Kathy at Christmas, Valentine's Day, and other special occasions. I've meant to do the right thing, but there have been times when I have forgotten, run out of time, or not paid enough attention to what I was buying, and hurt and disappointed my wife. I have made so many mistakes that I have written them all down and held myself up as a bad example to other men. I've told them to learn from me and do better than I did.

Being an object lesson is not as easy as it looks. It means that now that I've confessed my sins and repented of them, and led the congregation of men in the singing of hymns to take better care of our wives, I had better not commit the sins again.

Which is why I was on the Internet on February 8th to order flowers for Kathy for Valentine's Day. There was no way I could allow myself to forget. And, even though I was only doing the right thing, on time, like any responsible adult would do, I still felt a little proud of myself.

And I was still feeling proud that night when the phone rang and Kathy answered it. I could tell by what she said that it was the credit card company.

"Yes," said Kathy, "I made that purchase. From England, yes. Yes, that's fine."

Two months ago Kathy had bought a teddy bear from a shop in England. It was an expensive bear and the shop had agreed to charge her in installments. Last month, after the first installment, the credit card company called us and asked questions about our purchases to make sure someone hadn't stolen our card. It caught their attention when someone living in the United States suddenly made purchases in Britain. It was good to know that our credit card company was looking out for us.

Now they were calling again this month to check up on the next installment. Kathy told them this was a legitimate purchase. And, just to be sure, the agent at the credit card company asked other questions.

"Shell gas station? Yes, that's fine." She knows I buy gas on the way home from work.

"Il Restaurante D'Oro? Yes, that's fine." Kathy nodded. We both like Italian food and we ate there last week.

And then she looked at me and stood up on her toes, and smiled with the phone still pressed to her ear. "Well, I don't think I'm supposed to know about that, but, yes, I think that's okay."

Oh, damn! They must have told her about the flowers. Those were supposed to be a surprise! Couldn't I keep a secret for even eight hours? Didn't they train these people not to give away Valentine's Day purchases to people's spouses?

Kathy did not see any of these thoughts. I just smiled back at her, glad to see her glad. Happy February 8th, sweetie. Love you!

The agent, however, was not finished, and Kathy's expression turned a little more confused. "Victoria's Secret? Red satin camisole and tap pants? Um, absolutely." She looked at me, and I winked. Sometimes flowers aren't enough.

"Love butter? Love butter? That's Victoria's Secret, too, right? Oh, good. Yes, that too."

Well, I thought, if they were going to give away my Valentine's Day surprises, they might as well do them all.

"Four pounds of Max the Muscleman's Extra Potency

Protein Powder?" Now she squinted. I lifted both biceps in make-a-muscle pose to show her the purchase was for my new strength training regimen that I hadn't told her about yet.

"McDonalds? How much? Forty-three dollars? What the hell did he eat at McDonalds for forty-three dollars?"

Kathy listened to the agent say she didn't know the answer to that question, and I called out that it wasn't just me. I took a coworker too. And you couldn't eat the Protein Powder by itself. You had to mix it with something, like Diet Coke.

"Three ticket's to the Godz of Hard Rock summer tour? Well I hope he doesn't expect me to go. It sounds awful. And who's the third ticket for?"

The agent didn't know that either, and I cursed her again for ruining another surprise that I was going to spend all spring laying the groundwork for.

"Well let me ask you," said Kathy, "what would you think if your husband bought three tickets to a show he knows you wouldn't like? Wouldn't you want to know who the third ticket is for?"

I started to speak up to answer this question. I had thought Kathy's sister Marti, or her friend Wendy would want to go.

But Kathy turned her back to me and I could not get the words out. Now she was listening to the agent talk.

"Uh-huh, uh-huh. They do the dumbest things, don't they? Did I tell you that one year he bought a foam rubber neck pillow for Valentine's Day? What kind of gift is that? Oh, yeah, oh, yeah? You do? Really? Well, sure."

Kathy walked over and held out the phone to me. "She wants to talk to you. Her name is Suchita."

My eyes went wide and I shook my head no. Kathy held the phone closer and I pulled away. "I said no!"

Kathy stuck her tongue out at me and put the phone back to her own ear. "No, he won't do it. Yeah, figures. Anyway, all those purchases are legitimate. Why yes, the bear is very cute. I just love it. Was there anything else you wanted to tell me today? Okay, thank you so much for calling. Bye-bye."

The phone went beep when she pushed the off button. She looked at me. "Protein powder? Workin' on those muscles, are we?"

"No, I just like how it tastes. It comes in strawberry."

"Kind of like the shakes at McDonalds."

I shrugged. "I like strawberry."

"Mm," said Kathy. "I see. Could I make a suggestion?"

"Sure."

"Carry more cash with you."

I nodded. "That's a good idea," I said. It was a really good idea.

She stepped up and wrapped her arms around me. "Thank you for the flowers. I'm sure they're going to be beautiful."

I hugged her back. "You're welcome. Sorry they messed up the surprise."

"That's okay. I'll dry them so I can still look at them when you're taking your two mistresses to The Godz of Hard Rock."

"I was going to take you and your sister, but now that you mention it, do you suppose Suchita would want to go?"

Kathy lifted her head off my chest and looked up. "I doubt it. She already knows you too well."

Blissful Morning

My day is divided into two parts: before Kathy wakes up and everything else.

I don't need as much sleep as Kathy, which means that even when we go to bed at the same time I almost always get up an hour or two earlier.

I love the early mornings. I have a routine, and that routine consists mainly of doing whatever I want. Picture me, seated on the couch with the laptop on my lap. I read a bit of news - seems that politicians are fighting over money today, and the weather is likely to warm up for awhile and before it gets colder again. Then I work on whatever writing I happen to be working at the time, like t-h-i-s r-i-g-h-t n-o-w. There is nothing to disturb me, nothing making demands on my time, no one to say what I have to do instead of what I want to do. It is the most relaxing part of the day.

At least that's what it's supposed to be, but on some days there are obstacles between me and my blissful morning.

Take the cats. Last night they were right up against the bedroom door when I opened it and I could not get through without kicking them or waiting for them to move. This morning I waited. Other mornings I don't.

I usually give them fresh water when I get up, but this day the water had run out. We have a water cooler with bottles of water that need to be changed three or four times a week. I had to decide, should I change the bottle now? There was enough water for the cats, but it would be completely empty and no one else would get water until the bottle was replaced.

It should have been an easy decision – change the empty bottle – and it would have been simple if not for two things. First, I did not get up before dawn just to do household chores. Second, and this is the most important thing, changing the bottle makes a lot of noise. I would have to open the laundry room door and the sound would echo against the furnace and the washer and dryer, and changing the bottle would also make a loud squeak when I pulled it off the spindle, and the new bottle would make a popping sound when I put it on, followed by loud gurgling as the water filled the reservoir.

That's a lot of noise when the house is completely silent. Kathy was sleeping down the hall, and I didn't want to wake her. On the other hand, I wanted her to have drinking water and she wouldn't want to see the empty bottle sitting on the cooler. I asked myself, do I change the water and maybe disturb Kathy, or do I wait until she gets up and let her change it then?

When this happens the answer depends on how much important newspaper reading I have to do. There is a great deal going on in the world today and I consider it my responsibility as a citizen to stay informed. This duty takes precedence over changing the water, but if it's a slow news day, say a "New Panda at the Zoo" or "President Honors the Super Bowl Champs" kind of day, I'll risk waking up Kathy.

I changed the water this time, and went to the couch to begin a peaceful morning, or I would have if this hadn't been one of the days when a cat threw up.

Picture this: you're an ocean fish, not a glamorous fish like a tuna or a shark, but a small, ordinary fish just trying to have a good life. Then you get swept into a fishing net, beheaded on a freezing, stinking boat, chopped up and stuffed in a cat food can, and served on a paper plate to a pack of meowing cats. So far life isn't going the way you expected. If you happen to believe in reincarnation, you suspect this isn't going to be your last life on earth, and that in your previous life you probably made a few mistakes. Looking on the bright side, you think this is bad, but at least it can't get any worse.

Now imagine you've been in the cat's belly for a few hours and you're mostly digested and then the cat decides you're not a good fish to eat after all, and he rolls his shoulders forward and stiffens his neck and pukes you out onto the beige carpet.

And now, imagine how I felt about having to clean up the puke when I could be writing instead.

Oh well. Cats throw up, and that's just the way it is. I got out the cleaning liquid and a couple towels and took care of it.

Finally I arrived at the couch. I shut the living room door behind me, and I sat down to catch up on the news. The peace and quiet took me away and I wondered if it could get any more peaceful and quiet than this.

That's when I heard water running from the water cooler and I knew immediately what it was. I got up and opened the living room door and said in a loud whisper, *"Stop it!"*

One of the cats has figured out that if he gets on his hind legs and pulls down on the spigot he can get cold water whenever he wants. He lets it flow for awhile and drinks it out of the spillage trough.

His front paw was still on the spigot when he looked back at me and dropped down into a sitting position. Dude! You want some water? It's cold.

I could see the trough was almost full to overflowing. What could I do now? The cat already knew he's not supposed to drink from the cooler and he did it anyway. He's a cat, which means he never listens to advice from me, but I had to do something, right? I walked up to him, got on one knee and pointed my finger right at him.

"Do not *do* that!"

The cat looked back and me and blinked. Okay, dude. I was just trying to wash out the puke taste.

Good point. I know I wouldn't want to taste that all day.

He stood up and rubbed against me. Who wants to pet their favorite kitty?

I started to poke my finger again, but it only made me feel mean and foolish. "Okay, just one pet. C'mere, kitty."

I went back to the couch and continued with my quiet time. I opened my favorite news website and discovered that a mule had kicked down the fence of a local farmer and had wandered the streets of a small town for an hour before the sheriff's department took him back to the farm.

"We decided not to put handcuffs on him because he's always been a good mule before," said one deputy.

And in other news, a passenger train in Nigeria derailed and killed 108 people.

I continued to read about the new giraffe born at the zoo and the group skydive gone wrong. "The dive was supposed to spell 'Hi, Mom', but for these fourteen divers it only spelled Tragedy."

I heard a banging noise from down the hallway. I got up in a hurry. Stupid cats, what now?

There they were, taking turns leaping up and banging the bedroom doorknob.

One of them looked at the other. You can leap three feet into the air? Watch this, I can leap four and hit the knob twice.

I stepped in. "Guys, guys! I need you to be quiet, okay?"

One of the cats stopped to look at me while the other two were still jumping - *BANG.*

Okay, dude. You're the boss.

BANG!

"Now!"

Whatever, man. We're outta here. They all ran back up the hall and pretended to be scared of me.

I was afraid they had already woken Kathy up, but she did not wake up and I was able to go back to the couch. I thought this would be a good time to write a story about how Kathy always sleeps in, and I decided to start on it right after I read the article about a mutant strain of bacteria that whitens teeth.

The rest of the morning was perfectly quiet. No cats, no interruptions until dawn, when Kathy got up, the last and brightest beam of the sunrise.

She shuffled one foot-dragging step at a time from the bedroom, down the hallway, and into the kitchen. She turned the coffee pot on with one hand and scratched with the other.

"Coffee..." she said. "Uhhhhh"

I burst out of the living room to greet her. "Good morning, hotness!"

The sound of my voice broke her stride, and she turned in my direction and opened one eye a little wider to see who was talking. She sighed in disappointment.

"Was that you," she asked, "making all that noise?"

Your Big Ass Clogs My Living Room

Let me begin by saying my wife loves me very much. Having said that, she does not like everything I do.

Take, for example, the way I occupy our home with my physical presence. Kathy values organization and cleanliness, and I am a walking, talking, breathing, belching, slopping denial of every domestic belief she stands for.

If it were all up to me, I wouldn't need to clean the house every single day, and I wouldn't need to clean out the sink drains after every meal, and I wouldn't need to straighten the books so that their corners square with the edges of the coffee table. I could go on, but I think you get the idea. There are plenty of things Kathy thinks are important to a livable home that don't interest me.

It has always been that way. She first met me when I had been living alone as a bachelor for six years. I dwelled in an apartment with fleas in my fur and chicken bones stuck to the floor, and she lured me out of it, dressed me in long pants, and led me into the sunlight of mature married life.

The transformation is complete but it remains fragile. Think Frankenstein and his bride, or Tarzan and Jane. "Charlie wash dishes now. Charlie clean them goooood." I may be civilized, but I will never make it look as easy as Kathy.

One saving grace for Kathy is that I've spent most of my career working in office buildings, so that the messes I make at home are confined to the mornings, evenings, and weekend.

However, that changed recently. I've been assigned to a project where I can stay at home. I work from a laptop and communicate with the other members of the team with my cell phone, email, and instant messaging. The living room is now my office, and the commute is from one end of the house to the other.

At first Kathy was excited about the change. She would get to see more of me and wouldn't have to worry about me getting into a car accident during the commute. She would get my help around the house when she needed it, and she could plan the day better because she wouldn't have to wonder when I would come home.

I set up shop in the easy chair in the corner of the living room next to an end table with a drawer. My little office is complete and only five feet square, and at the end of the day when it's time to close up the office and go home all I have to do is stand up, take a big step to the left, and sit down on the couch next to Kathy.

It's a beautiful thing.

At least it's beautiful to me. Kathy, however, has started to have her doubts. Early in our marriage she created peace and order in her environment by teaching me how to eat with a fork and not throw my plate on the floor when the food was gone. Those were the good old days when every change was an improvement. Now it's more complicated. My disorganizing, disrupting, and disheveling nature hasn't gone away, and it's taken new forms that Kathy hasn't learned to fight yet.

The most obvious disruption is that I sit in the living room all day. It doesn't seem like it should be a problem, especially if I'm quiet, typing my little emails, writing my little computer programs, and not interrupting anyone else, but it's a problem for Kathy. When she enters the living room, I'm there. When she leaves the living room, I'm there. I'm there before she gets up, and I'm there all day until we go to sleep and I lie next to her in the bed. Sure, she likes to spend time with me, but all day and all night?

It's a big change for Kathy. She's used to having the house to herself during the day, and now she almost never does.

What makes it even harder is that I don't always sit quietly in the corner. My job requires me to speak with other people most of the day, and every time I speak with someone else, I influence what can and cannot happen in the living room.

Suppose the cell phone next to me rings.

"Kathy, could you mute the TV? Thanks, babe."

Kathy mutes the television. Now she can't listen to her show and instead she has to listen to me talk about why I haven't turned in my project planning documentation yet.

"...No, no, I'm working on it. Yes, I understand you can't run your global project status reports until I've submitted my updated numbers."

"...Of course I understand how important it is. I just have to talk to one more person to get the final iteration estimates."

"...By noon? If I can get the numbers by then. You'll hear back from me ASAP. Okay. Bye."

Kathy's thumb jumps on and off the mute button and she can never be sure she'll get to watch anything all the way through. Oprah is interviewing Sean Connery and Robin Williams for their new movie? It doesn't matter. I point to my cell phone and mouth the word *"talking"* and she has to mute the TV.

Not that it's all bad. Robin Williams might be easier to watch with the sound off. But Sean Connery without sound? Now that's unfortunate.

I try to make it up to Kathy with my own Sean Connery accent. "I'm sorry you had to turn down the telly, love." It is the worst Connery ever.

Kathy doesn't like it either. She makes a lemon-sucking face that doesn't go away when I wink at her with a Scottish accent.

Wenk.

Not only does she not get to watch TV, when we do watch TV she has to negotiate with me over what to watch, and we like very different things.

Kathy says, "How about QVC? It's Gem Fest week."

QVC is a shopping channel and it's *always* Gem Fest week. I don't like shopping, much less watching it on TV.

"No, how about C-SPAN?" I say. C-SPAN covers the national government, mainly the House of Representatives. It has a reputation for being boring but I think it can be extremely interesting.

"Nooo!" she says. "The Discovery Channel is doing a show on shark babies."

"You mean, like, human babies with shark teeth and fins?" I'm beginning to get interested.

"No, baby sharks."

"Oh....Nah. Shark is little, shark swims a lot, shark gets its first hundred teeth. Who cares?"

"Okay. There's a documentary on Egyptian pyramids."

"No." That channel shows nothing but pyramids and Nazis and I'm tired of it. I look through the listings. "Hey, the House Judiciary Committee is holding a hearing on tort reform. Let's watch that."

Kathy rolls her eyes. "You just want to watch them in their little outfits and all their makeup."

"*Tort* reform, not tart reform."

"Oh. It's a legal thing?"

"Yes."

"No way. How about a show on famous Victorian mansions?"

My cell phone rings and I put a finger over my lips to shush her. Victorian mansions, oh brother! "I told you I would get you the numbers as soon as I heard from the other guy. Okay? Okay? Okay then. Okay, bye."

As I'm talking on the phone I can hear Kathy talking to herself. "When you're not here I can watch jewelry and pyramids and mansions any time I want to. And I don't try to watch hookers on the government channel."

We don't always get along when it comes to the TV, and maybe it's for the best because we shouldn't watch TV anyway. But what really bothers her is the way I've organized the corner where I work.

Maybe "organize" is too strong a word. I sit in the chair in the corner of the room next to an end table. Kathy thinks of the end table the way she thinks of every surface in the room, as a place to decorate and add comfort and beauty to our living space. I think of it as my desk, and no desk of mine has ever been comfortable or beautiful.

Her attempts to make the office more livable have not gone well for her. The picture of our dog has to compete for space with my cell phone. I use the cinnamon scented candle as a stand for my stereo headphones. The lava lamp is hidden behind a cup of tea and bottle of water. Everything Kathy does to beautify the table is contradicted by something I do to make it functional.

And the cords! The ugliest thing of all is the power strip next to the chair with cords plugged into it going in all directions. I am surrounded by a web of cords.

Kathy never comments on them even though I know they irritate her. She vacuums the carpet several times a week, and when she pushes the vacuum cleaner near me she yells over it.

"Lift your feet!"

I lift my feet, holding the laptop on my lap, so she can vacuum under them.

Kathy takes her time. She makes sure to get all the dust under my feet.

"Lift the phone cord," she says.

I lift and she pushes the vacuum there.

"Now the laptop cord."

I put down the phone cord and pick up the laptop cord. I am still holding my feet up.

Funny how much dust Kathy can find under the laptop cord. Vacuuming...vacuuming...

"Move the power strip, please."

I reach out with one of my feet and push the power strip out of the way and Kathy vacuums there.

"Are you almost finished yet?" I ask.

"Pretty soon," she says. "There's a lot to vacuum under."

I know I get on her nerves sometimes, but I didn't think we had a real problem until I caught Kathy reading the classified ads in the morning paper.

"Why are you looking at the job postings?" She already had a job and wasn't looking for a new one. Then I saw she's looking at jobs for software engineers.

"You going to become a programmer, hon?" I asked.

She continued to look down through her reading glasses. "No."

"What then? A project manager, a business analyst, a software quality engineer?"

"No, I'm looking for a job for you."

"But I've got a job."

She pulled out a red felt pen and circled an ad, then put the paper down. "I think you would be able to move up faster if you worked somewhere else."

"What? I'm doing fine. I'm getting new projects and responsibilities. Things are going well here. Why would I want to go?"

"I just think you would do better if you had a job that gave you more new challenges and let you work outside the home."

"I get it," I said. "You're tired of having me around all the time."

"No, that's not it. I just think..."

The phone rang again and I held up my finger. "Shhh." I answered the phone. "No, I sent you the monthly hours, not the quarterly hours. That's what you asked for, remember?"

Kathy picked up the paper again and circled another ad.

Ladybug Kill, Kill, Kill

This is the holiday season and my wife and I have never been closer to fighting. She wants me to kill, even though it's almost Christmas, and I don't want to.

I blame it on the weather. We've had a very warm winter this year and that's why all the bugs that hatched in the summer have not died yet. In most years it would have taken only a day or two of deep frost and we wouldn't see another insect until May. But we didn't get those days and now all the bugs have sought shelter in our house.

Kathy doesn't like bugs in her house in any season. She fights them all year around, especially in the colder months when their numbers drop from millions to only hundreds and she thinks she has a fair chance of winning. If it's a bug and it's in our home, she squashes it. Or she makes me squash it. Kathy has assumed without question that if she wants bugs dead then I do too.

But I don't, not really. The reason is a combination of things. Part of it is the futility of it. If I kill a fly, there will be another one right behind it and I'll have to kill that one too, so what's the point?

Part of it is that killing things makes me uneasy, like it's not quite good for my soul. Did I mention that I've written poems about bugs, little haiku poems? I have. Like this one.

windows thrown open
the ant who crosses
the kitchen floor

Do you suppose the next thing I did was cock back my boot and give that ant what it deserved for coming into my kitchen?

No, I don't either.

And part of the reason I don't like to kill bugs is that it's just plain gross. Bugs make squishing noises and squish out their guts. It makes me nauseous.

Which is why it bothers me even more when Kathy asks me to kill bugs during breakfast. There I was, eating some cereal and looking forward to another happy day, when she said, "There's a fly on the ceiling. Kill it."

And I said, "I'm eating, sweetie."

And she said, "I don't want it to get away."

The fly was buzzing around and tapping into the overhead light. It wasn't going anywhere, so I said nothing, hoping Kathy would forget.

But she didn't. She pulled out a paper napkin and put on the counter in front of me. "I'm not tall enough to reach it."

"Sweetie, I'm eating, okay?"

"Honey, I want that fly gone. Flies spread disease and get in food. Do you want to eat that fly? Because that's probably what's going to happen if you don't take care of it right now."

I was starting not to want to eat at all, thanks to Kathy. I pictured the fly, dying of natural causes because I didn't murder it and dropping from the ceiling into the milk. Only I could prevent this. Kathy couldn't because she's too short to reach the ceiling and her arms are too stumpy.

(Kathy, who is reading this over my shoulder, has asked me to tell you that she is five-foot-eight and that her arms are perfectly proportional to the rest of her body - they are not stumpy - and that if I had wanted a wife who could reach the ceiling with a napkin then I shouldn't have married her.)

That's when I gave up and set my spoon down and picked up the napkin. I stood under the light and stared up at it and waited for the fly to stop moving. And waited. And thought about breakfast and how I could go back and eat it if Kathy hadn't stepped between me and the bowl with crossed arms.

Eventually the fly landed and I reached up and trapped it against the light. I pulled the napkin away with the fly inside and balled it up.

"Crunch it," said Kathy.

And I did. I squeezed the ball until I could hear a tiny crunching sound. I was still keeping on keeping on, but the fly's life was over. I threw the paper ball in the garbage.

Let's be fair. I don't like flies much either. Do I want them flying around during breakfast? Not really.

But I have to ask, does Kathy always have to worry about the bugs? Does she have to say something when there's one under the lampshade when we're on the couch snuggling? Does she have to point out the moth on the floor that's about to die anyway? Is there ever a time when we can all say, live and let live?

Apparently not. And the worst is the ladybugs.

I think there is nothing cuter than a ladybug. It's so round and it has that candy apple red shell with the little, itty, bitty, black spots. It even has "lady" in its name, like my grandmother or my second grade teacher. That is so precious. You just know God was having a cheerful day when He created ladybugs.

The problem with God where ladybugs are concerned is that He never creates just one ladybug so that I can appreciate it and forebear to kill it. No, He hatches them out of hidden nests by the bagful, and you can be sure that if you have seen one ladybug, and maybe had a teary moment about the beauty of life, there are a million more where that came from and you won't feel like weeping much longer.

Each of us has our level of tolerance for ladybugs. I can see a few hundred of them and hold some in the palm of my hand and feel their little pincers and talk to them from one end of the room to the other and blow them gently off my hand to their next destination. That's my level of tolerance.

Kathy's level of tolerance is this: none.

"What are you doing?" she said as I walked from this side of the room to the other side. She had come down the stairs.

"Nothing," I said.

"What's that? Is that a ladybug?"

"Um, no," I said. I pulled my hand in to protect my little red passenger.

"You were talking to it, weren't you?"

"I was talking to myself." I thought she would believe me because I talk to myself all the time.

But she did not believe me. "What were you saying to it?"

"I wasn't," I said.

"Charlie."

I sighed out my nose and looked at the ceiling then down again. "I said - I was saying how happy I was to carry her over to the window this fine Christmas morning." Did I mention it was Christmas? It was.

"Oh," she said, and she leaned forward to look at the little red insect in my hand. She put her eye up close and she said, "I'll get a napkin."

"No!" I said. "It's Christmas. Doesn't she look like a little Santa?"

"I don't care. It's a bug in my house, and it's gonna die."

She went to the kitchen and came back with the napkin and tried to hand it to me, but I wouldn't take it because I was singing to myself.

Silent night,

"Here's the napkin," said Kathy.

Holy night.

"Charlie."

All is calm,

"Charlie! Listen to me."

All is bright.

"Take it, Charlie."

Round yon Virgin...

And that's when she grabbed the ladybug out of my hand, opened the door, and flung it outside. "There," she said.

I stopped singing to myself, which is just as well because I couldn't remember the lyrics beyond Virgin anyway and would have had to start humming.

"Happy?" Kathy said.

I thought about this. At least the ladybug would have a chance to live. It was almost sixty degrees outside, so Kathy had shown a little Christmas spirit. "Yeah, I guess so," I said.

"Good," said Kathy. "Now take this napkin upstairs. There's a moth by the light in our bedroom."

I had given all my generosity to the ladybug and didn't have any fight left for a moth. "Okay," I said, and I started up the stairs.

"I want to see moth dust on your hands when you get back," she said. "There's no room at the inn for moths."

"I know," I said, and I went to stand under the bedroom light, waiting.

Love and Hug Therapy

My wife Kathy is my rock of support. She lifts up me up when I'm feeling down and gives me the strength I need in my times of worry. When I have troubles, she listens to me and tries to offer ideas for how to make the troubles better. No one does more than she does to help me see the big picture and appreciate that the difficulties of the moment are just a necessary step on life's journey. I love her for this. She's my best friend and I depend on her every day.

There is, however, more than one way to comfort a friend in need. There's the listening and helping way, like what Kathy does, and then there's my way, what I think of as love and hug therapy. I give Kathy a heapin' spoonful of it whenever the world gets her down.

Like yesterday, for example. She was not in a good mood. Kinda grouchy. I could see it as soon as she got up and began sending subtle signals.

"Charlie," she said, "Charlie, why are there grass clippings all over the kitchen floor? Get a broom and clean this mess up."

Those clippings got there, accidentally, when I took our mutual dog for his morning walk, and he walked through the grass and brought in a couple flecks with him. Aren't dogs silly?

Some husbands would have reacted negatively to Kathy's tone, but I took it as an opportunity to make her feel better. I walked up to her and wrapped my arms around her. "Hey, sweetie," I said into her ear.

See that? Love and hugs.

She didn't seem to absorb the healing right away. Even though I could feel the change in her mood, to most people it would have looked like she stood there unyielding to my touch, and most people would have read too much into the way she turned her head so that her eyeball looked into my eyeball. "Broom," she said. She did not blink.

"Right," I said. "Broom," and I went to get the broom and sweep the bit of grass on the floor, but before I did I squeezed her even harder and kissed her cheek and said "Loooovee you."

I kept up the therapy for the rest of the day. When she asked me what we should have for dinner and I said chocolate cake and she said could I please get serious for once in my life, I reached out and stroked her hair and said, "You know, I love your hair." I stroked it again and again.

And when later in the day I put away the laundry and got absolutely none of her clothes in the right drawer of her dresser and she asked me if I knew anything about her after ten years of marriage, I took her hand and patted it and kissed it and said that after ten years of marriage I still love holding her plump hands.

And when she called out from the bathroom, as I was passing a quiet hour on the couch with my laptop, whether it was necessary for me to splash water over every last corner of the sink and not clean it up, I went to her and hugged her and pinched her cheek and said no bathroom could help but be clean and dry if she worked on it.

And when, after, at her request, I had dried the sink with a towel, I found her in the kitchen, making dinner. I turned her away from a bubbling pot and laid my cheek on the bridge of her nose where I have always found a comfortable resting place. "I love your nose," I said. "It's so springy." I nestled into it. I snuggled into it. "Love you," I said.

She responded to my touch by turning back to the pot to continue stirring. And that gave me the opportunity to circle my arms around her waist from behind and press my chin up to the nape of her neck. "Whatcha cookin'?" I said. "It smells real good."

"It's stew," she said. "Don't you have something else to do?"

"Something other than holding you? No, I don't." And that's when I started to rub her back and massage her shoulders.

"Go away, I'm cooking," she said.

"Okay," I said, and I patted her back twice for good measure. "I'll be over on the couch."

"Just go," she said.

"I'll be waiting for my stew." Another pat and a rub.

"I said *go*," she said.

"Okay," I said.

You might be thinking that she was still feeling poorly and that the love and hugs were not raising her spirits. And maybe they weren't, net yet. No, you can't expect quick results with love and hugs. You have to stay with it, sometimes for hours, sometimes for days, until her rocky soil starts to bear fruit.

It wasn't until we turned in for the night and got into bed that the fruit came. That was when she rolled over to face me and she said, "Good night."

"Good night," I said.

"Thanks for taking care of me today," she said.

"Sure," I said. "Hey, it's what I do."

She pulled a hand out from under the covers and pinched my cheek. "You know what really works, don't you?"

Besides love and hugs? I said, "What?"

"Chocolate." She pinched my cheek again, a little harder this time.

"Oh," I said. "Okay."

"And diamonds," she said. Now she patted my cheek kind of hard.

"Okay. Got it. Let's go to sleep."

"Good night," she said. She tugged my earlobe. She whispered in my ear. "Remember: chocolate and diamonds."

"I said good night," I said. "I'm sleepy, okay?"

"Dark chocolate."

"Got it," I said again, and this time I rolled over.

"Love you," she said. "Love *you.*"

"Love you too," I said. "Now go to sleep."

"Good night," she said.

"Good night."

Rejection...again

Every writer receives rejections. It's a fact of life, and the best thing a writer can do is to accept it and keep a positive attitude.

One of the things that's made it easier for me to handle the rejections I've received is that it follows a predictable routine: I submit one story and the editor replies with one rejection. The process might not be pleasant, but at least it's familiar.

That is, until recently.

I submitted one of my stories to a well-known publication and received a gracious rejection letter about a month ago. It was disappointing, but by the book. Done and done.

Then yesterday I received another rejection letter from the same publication for the same story.

"Can they really do that?" I asked Kathy.

She held up the envelope and raised an eyebrow.

Okay, I guess they can do that.

"What does it mean?"

"I think it means they don't want your story," said Kathy.

"But I already knew that. Why tell me twice?"

Kathy shrugged.

"Let's think about that for a minute. There must be a good reason... Aha! I think I've got it. Maybe someone else with my name wrote the same story and sent it in to the same place. Hmm?"

"I don't think that's very likely," said Kathy. "No one else would have written that story."

"Why, thank you!" I said.

"You're welcome."

"How about this: I submitted the story again, but in the *future*, and the response came back to me here in the present. Time travel - get it?"

"No," she said.

"Okay. Let me try again. We're here in the present, right?"

Kathy's eyebrow again. "Yes..."

"Well maybe later, in the future," I continued, waving my hand forward to indicate the future, "I would want to submit it again. Maybe I rewrote it or something to make it better."

"Again," she said, "not likely, but okay..."

"So I submitted it again, in the future, and somehow - somehow - I got that rejection letter today. Get it now?"

"Yes," said Kathy. "I understand." She opened up the envelope and pulled out the letter. "According to your theory, what date would they have put on the letter: the present date, or the future date?

I considered this. "That's an excellent question. What date does the letter say?"

Kathy looked at the letter. She had to squint without her reading glasses. "Last Tuesday," she said.

"That's very interesting. Maybe they knew we would be reading it again here in the present so they changed the date to last Tuesday. Or maybe the letter came from another dimension that's different from this dimension by five weeks. Eh? Makes sense, doesn't it?"

Kathy's eyelids descended. "Don't you have some writing to do or something?"

"Sure. Always. But what's that got to do with this other dimension we're talking about?"

"Maybe," she said, "you should go write and let me think about the other dimension for awhile, okay?"

"Sure thing, sweetie." I kissed her on the forehead and went to my desk to write this story. In a little while I'll go check to compare notes with her. I already have a couple more ideas about the other dimension that she'll want to think about.

Burning Embers

Kathy is the first and best editor of all my stories. As soon as I write something, I print it out and set it on the table next to where she sits.

And then I wait.

But I do not wait in silence. I will say something like, "I wrote a story for you to look at."

A few minutes or a few hours later I will say, "Did you have a chance to look at that story? Just asking."

And a little after that I'll say, "How's that story coming? No worries. Just wondering."

One time Kathy asked, "Does it have me in it? Because if it has me in it, and you're telling everyone again what a hag I am, then no, I haven't read it."

"Sweetie! No one thinks you're a hag. They think you're tough but fair, and that you have a big heart."

Kathy considered what I said, and I felt for a moment that my words had reached out to that heart and made it beat just a little bit faster.

She said, "So...I'm not in it, right?"

"No. It's one of my stories about children."

I picked up the story from the table and held it out to her. She took it from me and pulled out her reading glasses from the drawer, and she began to read.

I sat beside her on the couch and watched. I followed her eyes with my eyes as they scanned each page from top to bottom, and when she finished it I followed her hand as she set it down.

Just before she finished the last page, I said, "So what did you think?"

"Well..." she started.

"Yeah?" I could have dunked her in barbecue sauce and eaten her in one gulp.

"Well, there are quite a few typos."

I didn't care about that. For me, typ-os are synonymous with typ-ing. "Yeah, and?"

"And I was wondering about the haiku you started the story off with."

"Yeah?" This was one of my stories about kids growing up, and all of them start with a short poem called a haiku. For this story, the haiku was:

burning embers
a wildfire
under his boot

It would take several minutes to explain why the children's stories all have a haiku, and I don't want do divert us from Kathy's feedback for that long, so suffice it to say that it has to do with the parallel symmetries of the juxtaphors found in haiku and the dualistic tension between adults and children represented in the stories.

Kathy said, "I was wondering if it really adds anything to the story."

I said. "Yes, I think it does," and explained the parallel symmetries. Kathy listened, and when, as it happened more than once, I could tell by the way her mouth hung open that she didn't fully understand what I was saying, I repeated it until she did understand.

When I was finished, Kathy said, "Oh. That's more than I read into it. I thought it was just a story about a boy on a camping trip."

"It is," I said. "And it's more than that."

"Well, *yeah*. It's about a boy who almost starts a forest fire while his parents are sleeping." she said.

"Well, kind of."

"The boy gets a stick, puts it into the campfire until it's burning, and waves it around until a bush catches on fire. Isn't that about starting a forest fire? Because that's what I read into it."

"Yeah, I suppose, but did you like the description of how he snuck out of his tent - "

"The part about how loud the tent zipper was - that was good."

"Uh-huh, and how when he had it all the way unzipped he could see a million stars."

"I read through that part pretty fast," Kathy said. "It was fine."

"Oh," I said. I like to think my stories are meant to be savored, not skipped through, but never mind. "Anyway," I said, "what about how the campfire was steeped with cooling orange embers and how Jeremy tiptoed to the edge of the campfire to find the straightest, most perfect stick, and how he probed the fire with his stick to find the hottest coals, like a tongue jabbing at the empty spot where a baby tooth once was?"

Kathy picked up the pages and held them out to me. "Would you like to read the whole thing out loud?"

"No, I was just wondering what you thought of that part."

"It was fine too."

"Okay," I said, but I was really thinking, what was the point of letting her read my story if she won't appreciate its most creative passages?

"So getting back to what I was saying," said Kathy, "the kid is whipping his stick around outside in the dark -"

"*Tracing the night sky with streaks of orange magic...* Right, go on."

"Can I finish?"

"Of course," I said. "Please continue."

"Why didn't his mom and dad make him go back to bed?"

"They were sleeping. And he was doing it very quietly."

"Yeah, okay. That reminds me of another thing." She flipped through the pages until she found a particular passage. "You wrote, *His mother and father had their own tent, and they zipped their two sleeping bags together into one big bag for maximum comfort.*"

"Yeah?" I said. "What's your point?"

"Maybe Mom and Dad weren't really sleeping, and they didn't send Jeremy to bed because they, um, had better things to do." She bit her lip.

"Kathy! It's a children's story. Why do you have to say that?"

"I don't know, I'm just saying..."

"That's *not* what was happening. The point of the story is the boy and his stick."

Kathy looked at me. "Isn't it always?"

"Stop that! Get back to the real story."

"Yeah, whatever," said Kathy. "So he sets a bush on fire - no hidden meaning there either, I'm sure - and a forest ranger just happens to appear in time to stamp it out." She put the pages down. "Am I supposed to believe that?"

"Smoke jumper," I said. "Not forest ranger."

"What?" said Kathy.

"He wasn't a forest ranger. He was a smoke jumper."

"Same difference," said Kathy.

"No it isn't. Smoke jumpers put out fires, not forest rangers."

"Fine. And he just happened to be around when Jeremy set the bush on fire?"

"Yes."

"You didn't say how he got there."

"I know I didn't," I said. "That's called creative omission. You don't need to know how he got there, so I didn't tell you. He was just there."

"Let me see if I understand," said Kathy. "You had time to tell me what Jeremy's tent zipper sounded like, but you didn't bother to explain how a stranger showed up in the middle of the forest at just the right time?"

"That's right. You see, it's not how many details you put in a story. It's which ones you put in. The zipper was important because it conveyed context - the wonder Jeremy felt at that moment. Where the smoke jumper came from - or what his hair color was, or what college he went to, or what he had for lunch - wasn't important, so I left it out."

"Why would I, as a reader, keep reading if the story doesn't make any sense?"

"To find out what happens," I said.

Kathy squinted. "Okay..."

"And to increase your perspective."

Now Kathy's eyes squinted all the way shut. She inhaled and exhaled through her nose twice, and opened them again back to a squint. She ruminated some more and tried to find the perfect words, and I waited to hear them.

She said, "Here's my perspective. No one is going to believe he showed up from nowhere, and no one is going to believe he put out a whole bush on fire just by stomping on it."

"He's a smoke jumper!" I said. "It's what he *does*."

"Okay...what's the smoke jumper's name, Charlie?"

"It doesn't matter! He crushed the fire with his boots. That's what counts."

"So he never says, 'By the way, my name is Steve, what's your name?' or anything like that?"

"No."

"Why does he just stomp out the fire and leave? Why don't they talk to each other?"

"Oh, no, they do talk," I said. "That's the whole point of the story."

"I didn't see any talking. He just left."

"No, no, no." I picked up the pages and found the paragraph I was looking for. I read, "*Once the fire was extinguished, they stopped and looked at each other, the man at Jeremy, and –* "

"Steve –" said Kathy.

"Shh! ...*the man at Jeremy, and Jeremy at the man. They held the moment for a long time, and in that moment, in which there was no more fire, they understood each other. Jeremy nodded, and so did the man. And then he stepped backward and disappeared into the darkness that he himself had just created, and was gone.*"

"And...?" said Kathy. "They didn't say anything."

"But they communicated. The absence of words only makes it more powerful."

"But they didn't say anything!"

"Yes they did. It's all right there in the story."

"I don't get it."

"Okay. You kind of have to put it together with the ending. See if this helps." I read, "*Jeremy sat alone with his lifeless stick that had once been burning. He was silent. But then he looked upward and saw that, up there in the sky, were a million brilliant stars, themselves burning like the embers of a million distant campfires. Jeremy saw this and blinked, and then he went back into his tent, drew the zipper back down, and was gone.*"

I looked up from the manuscript and paused to hold the mood. If I had been wearing reading glasses I would have taken them off. "See?" I said.

"No," said Kathy. "When I read a story, I want to know who's in it and what happens, bam, bam, bam! I don't think it's too much to ask for the characters to have names, and if it's supposed to mean something, I don't think it's too much to ask to get a little help understanding it."

"It's metaphorical. Like the haiku. They each have resonance in themselves and they resonate with each other."

"I didn't get the haiku either."

"Oh," I said. "Then I guess you shouldn't be reading children's stories."

"I guess not," she said.

I set the pages back down. "Well, thanks for the advice. I always find it very helpful to improving my stories."

"You're welcome. I'm glad I could help."

And that seemed to be all there was to say, until Kathy said, "I was wondering: you seem to be fascinated with zippers all of the sudden. What's that about?" She looked at me, and I think she winked.

"No!" I said. "Stop it. It's a children's story."

"I'm just saying."

"Well stop saying it."

"No, because unlike some people, I don't do all my communicating through haiku and silence!"

And at that moment there was, in fact, a moment of silence, followed by a proposition by one of us, who shall remain nameless, to zip our sleeping bags together. We looked at each other, I at her, and she at Steve - I mean me - and then we withdrew into our tent and were gone.

Scared

"I want to go outside," said Kendall.

Kendall, her mom Wendy, Wendy's mom, Kathy, and I sat around a wooden table at The Pelican Sports Bar with ketchup-streaked plates and half-empty glasses of lemon ice tea. Televisions in every corner showed Michigan up against Notre Dame 6-0 at the end of the first quarter. Kendall had finished her kid burger, colored all the pictures in her crayon book, and had reached the limit of her patience for listening to grown-ups talk.

"I'm going to the lake to get warm," she repeated. "It's cold in here." The Pelican sits next to a lake. She got up from her chair and started for the door. The sun was shining and it was a very blue September day.

"No, honey," said Wendy. "Go where I can see you."

"I want to go to the lake!"

"No, honey. Go where I can see you. How about going on the deck? It's warm out there." She pointed to the porch where customers were eating outside under sun umbrellas. "Go out there."

Kendall shrugged and skipped out the door that opened onto the deck. I watched through the window as she walked from one end of the wooden porch to the other - bored, bored, bored.

I turned back to the others. "You know," Wendy told us, "I let Kendall go to her first football game by herself."

Kathy said, "Wow. I don't think my mom let me go any-where until I was twelve or thirteen."

"Well, she went with a friend and there were other people from her class there. But they weren't all sitting together."

"How was it?" Kathy asked.

Wendy laughed and looked down at her hands. "Ehhh, you know," she said. "It was a long two-and-a-half hours waiting for her to come home. I mean, she had her cell phone. She would have been okay...but, you know..."

The rest of us looked down. Of course she would be fine out on her own with her friends. But, you know...

"I almost called her, you know, just to ask her what the score was." Wendy smiled. "But I didn't want to embarrass her."

We all shook our heads. No, of course we wouldn't want to embarrass her.

"Or I could have gone to the game and sat in the back stands where she wouldn't see me. That would have been okay, wouldn't it?"

We nodded. Of course it would, as long as Kendall didn't know.

"But I didn't. I stayed home and cleaned the house. Lord knows I never have enough time by myself."

I saw Kendall out of the corner of my eye. She had come in from outside and was sneaking up on Wendy with her fingers raised in claws. She pounced on her mom and roared, "*Eeeeyah!*"

Wendy hardly flinched at all. She patted Kendall's hand and asked, "Are you warm now, punkin?"

"Mom, you're supposed to be scared!"

Wendy said, "I'm sorry, sweetie. You have to try harder than that."

Kendall sighed. "Oh, fine!"

Wendy's mom looked up at Wendy and back down at her plate, smiling to herself.

Kendall sat back down and gnawed on the last of her pickle slices. Bored, bored, bored.

Middling Management

I have held only one job since arriving in Michigan, working for a consultancy that specializes in working with software systems. Companies that need to create new systems or combine multiple older systems into a shiny new package come to us.

Even though I have had one job, I have held several titles that represent a rise in responsibility and a strong upswing in my career.

Let's review.

I was first hired as a developer, meaning my primary job was to write code for the software systems, and even though I was not specifically hired to provide leadership, I was made the technical lead on my first assignment. I wrote most of the code and also directed the work of the three other developers.

I took a career detour on my next two assignments, working again strictly as a developer.

After that came the assignment from which I didn't look back. I worked as a project manager and business analyst. I led a small team, similar to the first assignment, except that I did not write any code, was not expected to write any code, and as far as the technical lead on the project was concerned, was encouraged not to write any code. The transition to management was complete.

On the next project I was asked to be the project manager leading a team of eight other people. That was already a big assignment, and then I was asked to serve as the engagement manager for the account, meaning I was responsible for managing profitability, not just the successful completion of the work.

There was even more to come. The company was growing so fast that my boss had trouble keeping track of all his projects, so he created a new position called regional manager for people who oversee multiple accounts, and assigned me to one of these positions. I had a territory, and I was not just management now – I was middle management.

Soon after the promotion I was asked to take over a new account called Rejoice Industries that had been started by the other regional manager, a colleague named Evan. He was looking to transition it to me so that he could focus on developing other clients. My job would be to monitor the team's progress, mentor its new project manager, and look for other opportunities to sell our services to Rejoice. Evan called a meeting for me to meet the development team and get started on the right foot. He provided the address and set the meeting for 10:00 AM the next morning.

I did what anyone going to a new place would do. I put the address into Yahoo Maps and got driving directions. I looked them over and they seemed straightforward. Rejoice, it turns out, is located in a suburb of Detroit called Wiedlin Meadows. That's a pretty name, I thought. And it's a meadow!

I set out the next morning with plenty of time to spare, looking forward to a working with a new account and passing on hard-earned experience to a new project manager. Just imagine how much better the new project would go than my first project because of how much smarter I was now. The thought of it made me rev the car engine a little harder as I drove off. Kathy's goodbye kiss was still warm on my lips.

I followed the directions down I-75 and got off at the exit they indicated. The directions led me through a residential neighborhood, down narrow side streets, then even narrower side streets with cars parked on either side. This was not the trip through a business district that I was expecting.

Let me talk for a minute about Wiedlin Meadows. The name doesn't convey the same aesthetic as the actual place. The name suggests suburban planning, with business courts, abundant trees, tall buildings with tinted glass, and places to get same-day dry cleaning and four-dollar lattes. In other words, clean and modern, if a little soulless and over-manicured.

Wiedlin Meadows, it turns out, isn't like that at all. I drove by houses without paint, doors, or glass in the windows, open areas that might have been parks if they weren't overgrown with dead shrubbery and strewn with empty bottles, and teenagers wandering the streets in the middle of the day. Wiedlin Meadows is the kind of place that makes you think about carjacking and doesn't seem to have much appreciation for the valuable skills of a regional manager.

I saw all this out of one eye while using the other eye to follow the directions. I was led, finally, to a busy four-lane street. I hoped it was Bellemont Avenue, because that's where Rejoice is located, but I couldn't tell because there were no street signs. That's one of the funny things about Michigan. In Michigan the street planners are great about putting up signs to show the name of the upcoming cross-street, but don't put up signs to show what street you're on. More than once while driving to a new place I've had to turn off a street just so I could find a sign to tell me what street I had just left.

Anyway, I could tell I was lost, so I pulled over at a local bank to look at the driving directions and ask for help. When I looked carefully at the piece of paper I could see the problem. The directions did not lead to Rejoice. Rather, they led to the center of the zip code in which Rejoice is located. Apparently Yahoo did not know where to find Rejoice and I would have to find the rest of the way without its help.

I asked myself, what would a regional manager do now? And then I had the answer.

The next step was to ask directions at the bank. I would have preferred to get out of the car and walk inside the bank to talk to a teller face to face, but I couldn't because the bank didn't have a front door, only a drive-through, presumably to protect the safety of the people inside.

I drove into the drive-through and leaned out the window to talk into the speaker attached to a metal pole. I asked the teller, who I could see through the window thirty feet away, in a slow and clear voice how to get to Bellemont Avenue. She conferred with a co-worker and leaned into her microphone to tell me that I needed to turn left on the big street and keep going until Six Mile, and take another left. I said thanks, and set off.

I called Evan to tell him I was running late and would be there shortly. It was 9:50, and I thought I had a good chance of being only ten minutes late now that I knew where I was going.

It turned out the big street was Edsell, one of the major thoroughfares north of Detroit. I had gotten off the freeway near Eight Mile and was now driving south with the city's skyscrapers on the horizon, so it seemed reasonable to me that Six Mile would be just ahead.

It wasn't. I drove for three miles past liquor stores, check cashing stores, gas stations, and used car dealerships without passing any Mile sign at all, until finally I reached Ronson University and knew that if there was a Six Mile, I had missed it. I turned off of Edsell and pulled over at a drug store to ask directions.

Three ladies gave me directions that basically said to go back the way I came on Edsell until I saw signs for Bellemont. I told them thanks and got back in the car.

I thought I knew how to get back to Edsell, but when I drove to where I thought it was, it wasn't there.

I ended up making a big circle around the University, looking for Edsell, so I could find Bellemont Avenue, so I could get to Rejoice. The closer I got, it seemed, the farther away I was.

I pulled over again to talk to a parking lot attendant who pointed me back to Edsell, and, relieved, I drove back the way I came, past the bank, and past Eight Mile. There was still no sign of Bellemont, so I pulled over for a third time at a used car dealership to ask for directions. Car dealers know the neighborhood, right?

The man in the office at the dealership didn't know where Bellemont Avenue was, and neither did the guy he asked sitting behind the other desk. He said he would look for it on Yahoo Maps, which he did, very slowly. He moved the mouse on the screen a little bit and called up a browser and looked like he was going to type something in, and then he pulled his hands back.

I offered up the starting point, giving him the URL for Yahoo Maps. He didn't seem to hear me the first time and kept rolling the mouse around and around, as if he could rub the answer out of the screen. A lot of thinking was going on, but not much helping, and I began to feel impatient again.

I leaned forward a little more and repeated the URL, and this time he heard me.

"Oh, do you know computers? Do you want to try this?" He stood up and offered me the chair, and I thanked him with a smile and sat down. I had the Yahoo Maps page up in about ten seconds. I performed a search, found Bellemont Avenue, and I could see how to get to it from the dealership.

I turned to thank him and he said, "Would you like me to print that for you? It'll just take a second."

The directions were easy to remember and I didn't really need the print-out, but I didn't want to be rude. "Sure," I said. We waited together for another couple minutes for the printer. It was one of those one-page-at-a-time printers. The engineers who designed it had given up printing speed to make it small enough to fit easily on a desk. The dealer must have realized it wasn't the fastest printer in the world because he held the corner of the page as it came out to make it print just a little bit faster, and finally pulled it completely free and handed the map to me.

"There you go, sir."

I thanked him and headed back out to the car. My impatience had lifted and I was already looking forward to getting to Bellemont Avenue. It was a clear, warm, late-winter day. The sun was shining and I knew where I was going again. Sure, I had lost an hour, but if this was the worst the day the day could offer, everything would turn out all right.

The enthusiasm did not last long. According to the map Bellemont Avenue was supposed to be just on the other side of I-75, and yet when I crossed over I-75, it wasn't there. I drove another mile just to make sure - nope, no Bellemont Avenue. No one, and I mean no one, seemed to know where Bellemont Avenue was: not the car salesman, not the parking lot attendant, not the three ladies as the drug store, not Yahoo Maps, and sure as the day is long, not me. What could I do now?

I pulled over at a gas station and called Evan. Unlike when I first called him, I knew where I was, and he was able to give me the name of the exit to take and how to get to Rejoice.

I drove back to I-75, and it didn't take me long to realize that even though I now had the street name of the exit, I didn't know whether to go north or south. I hadn't thought to ask Evan. I consulted my gut, and it told me to go north.

It turns out a man's gut doesn't always know the right answer. I realized after driving north for awhile, passing exists I knew were beyond the right exit, that it had given me bad advice. I turned back south, passed the place where I had gotten on the freeway, and continued directly to the exit Evan had given me. In fact, I followed his directions all the way to Rejoice without any trouble at all. It could not have been easier. If I had gotten off at the correct exit in the first place, I could have been 30 minutes early rather than 90 minutes late.

I figured out later that the street address I had been given to Rejoice was missing the first digit and Yahoo Maps had done the best it could by putting me in the middle of the same zip code. I should be thankful because if the exact address had existed on the map, I would have ended up a hundred blocks away from Rejoice.

But no matter: I had arrived. I called Kathy to tell her I was safe and called Evan to have him meet me at the front door, then got out of the car to go inside. It had been a long time since I had been so relieved to get where I was going.

The door to the visitor's lobby was locked - this was still a dangerous neighborhood. Evan walked up and swung it open.

"Hey, man," he said. "Come on in and get signed in."

"Hey," I said. We walked over to the reception desk to get me a visitor's badge and he told me what had happened so far. The team was meeting with the Rejoice project manager and going over all the details needed to get the project off to a good start. So far so good, I thought, routine stuff. I ought to be able to listen in and make a contribution.

Evan led me to the conference room and I took a seat as if I belonged there. "Everyone, meet Charlie Close," he said. "He's the regional manager for this account."

The man on my left was the first to speak. "I'm Wendell. Did you get a good look at Wiedlin Meadows?" He smiled.

I laughed, maybe too much. "Yes," (hee, hee), "I sure did." (hee, hee, hee)

Okay, I might have giggled like a girl. That's what I do sometimes after a stressful situation. But you should have felt my handshake. It was firm and manly and very managerial.

I didn't feel quite as awkward after I looked around the table. They were all laughing at my roundabout journey to get here and they were all dressed much like I was. Except, that is, the grey-haired man at the head of the table who looked very professional in a business suit. This, I thought, must be the Rejoice manager. He stood up and leaned over to shake my hand. "Curtis," he said.

Ah. This wasn't the Rejoice manager. This was the project manager from my company who was going to lead the project. I was here to be introduced as his boss. Nice suit, Curtis.

The actual Rejoice manager was Wendell, who picked up where he left off before I came in. And from that point on, I was in my element: a project with software and hardware and a goal to accomplish.

Well, actually, I wasn't *quite* in my element. In the past I had always been one of the people in the room directly responsible for coming up with a solution to whatever the problem was, whether it was developing software myself or leading a team of other developers. My ideas were always in the middle of the project and I was expected to get my hands dirty.

Not so here. This time my job was to make sure the team, led by Curtis, had what it needed, and to address any concerns Wendell might have. My role was supposed to be more high-level than that of any of the other people in the room, excepting Evan, who was transferring his job to me.

Most of my job, I realized, consisted of listening. What did Curtis or the developers miss, what was Wendell thinking about that wasn't apparent on the surface? I was not supposed to say much. The only problem was, how was I supposed to look like I was contributing if I didn't say anything? I was a pretty smart guy, despite not knowing how to get around in Wiedlin Meadows, and I wouldn't want anyone to think otherwise. I had to establish credibility as a manager, which is why I chipped in comments like these.

"That task might take longer than it sounds on paper. Have you incorporated the extra risk into your plan?"

...and...

"It's critically important to get off to a strong start. Otherwise it can be awfully hard to finish strong, like I know we all want to. Right, guys?"

...and...

"Are you comfortable with the proposed deployment strategy, Wendell? We can always refactor it to give greater weight to the weakest links in the dependency chain."

That's what management is for, I realized, to be cautious and leaven the conversation with the wisdom of experience. I gave them all a lot to chew on, judging by the looks around the table, and I could feel I was getting into the swing of things.

And so, with plans made and Wendell duly reassured, the meeting ended. The plan was to go to lunch and come back for a demonstration of the software system that the project was intended to enhance.

Lunch did not entirely perpetuate the image of competent strength I had projected in the conference room. For example, I dropped my badge on the ground as the group of us walked from our cars to the chicken wing restaurant. The badge had one of those metal clips that popped easily off my belt. Alex, one of the new team, asked if I was trying to quit already as he held the badge up for me to see.

And then there was the way, after we sat down, I was invited to tell the team a little bit about myself and was cut off in the middle of the first sentence. Alex had not returned from the bathroom yet and I should wait until he got back so he could hear it too.

And then there was the moment I dropped the plastic fork when I tried to unwrap it from its cellophane. I grabbed another fork and I don't think anyone saw the first one disappear.

And then there was the way I accidentally flicked Caesar salad onto my pants while trying to corner it on the plate. Maybe no one saw that either, and even if they had, I know plenty of middle managers who flick their salad. Caesar salad dressing has a lot of calories and it's healthier to wear it than to eat it.

After lunch we all got back into our cars and returned to

the office. We took the route back along Edsell Avenue near Eight Mile. Rejoice, as I could see by all the buildings I had passed by three times earlier in the day, is not far from where I had first gotten off the freeway. I had been within ten minutes of Rejoice almost all morning and the scenery now looked comfortingly familiar.

The next mishap occurred when we tried to get back in the Rejoice building. Thankfully it didn't happen to me this time. It happened to Alex. Never mind that I caused it to happen to Alex.

The side door at Rejoice had an automatic lock that required a badge to be presented before it would open, which would have been no problem, since we were all photographed and given badges this morning - that is, except for me, since I had arrived late and still had a visitor's badge.

When I presented my badge to the door, the door did not open. Visitor badges do not open doors.

"No problem," said Alex. "I'll use mine." He swiped his badge at the door and I walked in. It was a revolving door designed to let only one person through at a time.

As I was passed through, another member of our group named Bill leaned over to Alex and said, "You know you're not going to be able to get in now."

"What?" said Alex.

"You can only use your card once," said Bill. Now that he said it, it was obvious. The security system thought Alex was already inside so it wouldn't let him through again. The security system was smarter than Alex had thought.

But he tried anyway. He swiped his badge and pushed on the door. It didn't budge, and we all laughed. Even I laughed, quietly, on the inside - the inside of the building, that is. Looks like someone didn't plan for all the contingencies, eh, Alex?

We resolved the problem with a phone call to the reception desk using the phone hanging by the door, and once we were all inside we went to Olivia's cube to see the demo. She was the Rejoice employee who knew the most about the system we were going to work on. She was going to give a demo so that our development team could see it for themselves and ask questions. My job, like at the earlier meeting, was to listen for places to make knowledgeable comments.

That's what I did for several minutes. It was quite interesting and I did not feel the need to say anything at all. The other members of the team asked questions, and Olivia answered them, and I stood back and paid attention to the situation as a whole - from a higher level, you might say.

Being at this higher level, I did not immediately hear the phone ring in the cube next to Olivia's, nor did I see the occupant of the cube stand up and look around the room in all directions with the phone still pressed to his ear. I was busy listening for project opportunities, risks, and mitigations and did not notice the man with the phone until I heard a single word.

"...Toyota..."

That caught my ear. It so happens I drive a Toyota. I looked in his direction and he, spotting my moving head out of the corner of his eye, turned to me. He said, as if repeating what was being spoken into his ear, "Someone's parked a Toyota in the visitor lot? And it's locked and still running?"

How interesting. "What color is the car?" I asked. I was only curious. He nodded and repeated my question into the phone. While we waited for the answer, I reached into my pockets to confirm I had my car keys. I always keep them in the left front.

They were not there.

Evan had noticed the new conversation by this time, and watched as I checked my other pants pockets and the pockets in my jacket. No keys.

"I think it's mine," I said to the guy with the phone.

"Dude!" said Evan.

"I've got to go," I said. I was kind of laughing, as if to say, can you believe this?

"Okay," said Evan. He was smiling too and slapped my back.

"Tell them I'll be down in a minute," I said. The man with the phone nodded.

I stepped smoothly away from the demo and, once out of sight, double-timed it to the reception desk where the receptionist and two men with tool belts were waiting for me.

"Hi," I said. "My car is the one running outside."

"All right, then," said the receptionist. "I'm going to have you follow these gentlemen outside so they can unlock your car."

"Okay."

"And, sir, you're parked in the area reserved for our clients. They pay our bills every month so we need to keep that area clear for them."

"Yes, ma'am," I said. "I didn't know."

"I understand, so if you could park farther down, behind the red lines, I'd appreciate it." She smiled at me.

"Sure thing," I said.

"Because that's how we noticed your car in the first place. The president of the company walked by and didn't recognize your car. We've been looking all over for you."

The president saw my car and started the hunt for me? Oh, man! Who *didn't* I impress today? "I'm very sorry. I won't do that again."

"That's fine. Follow these gentlemen, please, and park behind the red lines."

The three of us went out and I stood by as they broke into my car using two tools: a rubber wedge to pry open the door half an inch, and a metal shim to pull open the lock. I had thought the car was reasonably well-protected from theft. It's not. Anyone who knows what they're doing can steal it in less than three minutes.

They talked during the break-in. "I think he owes us a nice dinner, Ron," said one of the men to the other. He meant me. "You like steak?"

"Sure do," said the other. "And lobster's good too."

I laughed. There was that giggling girl again. "Yeah," I said. "You guys are earning dinner now. I could have been in big trouble. At least there's still gas in the car."

"This car get pretty good mileage?" asked Ron.

"Yeah, pretty good" I said. "About 32 on the freeway." And about ten hours on the parking lot.

"Yeah, not bad, not bad."

In a moment the first man had the car door open and I was able to shut off the engine and retrieve the keys. I dropped them into my pocket and double-checked they were there.

"You guys looked prepared for this," I said. "You have to get into cars often?"

The first man shrugged. "About once a week."

I felt a little better. My mistake wasn't as crazy as I had thought, although I bet not everyone was noticed by the company president.

I thanked them again and when they left I moved the car to the other side of the red line, a hundred feet farther from the door. I didn't mind because the beautiful morning had turned into a warm late-winter afternoon, one of the best since the fall. I was tempted to skip the rest of the day and stroll outside for an hour or two. But no, I had responsibilities. Someone had to lend a firm hand to the demo to make sure all the relevant information was conveyed, and if I didn't do it, who would?

I reached out to open the front door, and that's when I realized I had lost my badge again. It wasn't on my belt like it was supposed to be.

Uh-oh. I had dropped it somewhere.

I wasn't worried because I knew I had it when I parked the car. I retraced my steps and found it lying next to the car door on the driver's side. This time I put it in my pocket.

No problem. No one else saw. Okay then? Okay. Time to go back in there and make it happen.

I reentered the building and returned up the stairs and down the hall, back to where the rest of the group was assembled. My path was straight and confident right up to, and including, the moment I encountered the first locked door. I pulled out the badge between my thumb and forefinger and presented it without hesitation to the sensor, and the door did not open.

Okay, champ, now what?

Well, I didn't exactly know. But what I did know, and know still today, is that effectiveness in the face of uncertainty and difficulty is one the distinguishing characteristics of a leader, and the higher a leader aspires to go, the more uncertainty he will face, up to, including, and beyond an occasional locked door. A leader must accept such challenges and take action.

And that is why, with the locked door between me and my goal of rejoining the demo, I looked around for help. I looked to the right and saw nothing, and to the left, certain that someone nearby must have a badge that could let me through.

And, just like I knew there would be, there was help in the distance to the left. I looked to the woman standing there and she looked back at me, and I jabbed a finger at the door and shrugged, and she pointed at the door and held up her badge and gave me a question mark look, and I nodded and gave her the thumbs-up signal. She nodded and walked over to me.

"Hi," she said and swiped her card and opened the door for us both to pass through.

"Hi," I said. "I'm looking to get back to Curtis's desk."

"Oh sure, I can take you there," she said and introduced herself as Jodie.

I said I was pleased to meet her.

As we walked back toward the demo she said over her shoulder, "Are you one of the new consultants working on the conversion project?"

I told her I was.

"I thought so. You haven't filled out any of the forms or gotten a badge, have you?"

"No. I came a little late." I was the only one on the team who didn't have an official badge yet. Just ask Alex.

"I thought so. Well I'm going to need you to come this way to get a form to fill out. We need to process you in, since we missed you this morning."

"Oh, okay," I said. It just so happened that Jodie was the department administrator. What were the odds of that? See how everything works out for the best when you move with confidence? Not only did I get where I was going, I also was able to get caught up with the administrative preliminaries that come with joining a new project.

"You're sure you have a minute?" she asked.

"Yes I do. I was called away from the others to get into my car and they don't know when I'll be back anyway."

She stopped and turned to me. "Oh! Were you the one who left his keys running in the locked car in the customer-only part of the visitor parking lot?"

"Yes, ma'am."

"Oh, wow! They were looking all over for you."

"Yes, ma'am, I'm sure they were."

She led me back to her desk, gave me a piece of paper to fill out, and walked me over to Curtis, Evan, and the others. The demo was still in progress.

"You give the form to Evan when you're done," she said, "and he'll give it to me, okay?"

"Yes, ma'am," I said. She departed and I returned to the demo.

After the demo, we all got together in a meeting room to discus the work we had to do and the challenges in front of us, and I felt I had returned to a more comfortable position. I could ask questions and use earlier experiences to guide the project in the right direction. Did they, I asked, have the equipment they needed, computers, desks, and such? Did the team have access to the people they needed? Did they have the client's clear definition of a successful project and a way to measure whether we succeeded? Had they taken steps to run the project according to the standards of our company? The more questions I asked, the more I realized that my experience could help them and that I was being given the opportunity to manage other teams for a reason.

Moments like these didn't come often, when all the months of laboring on projects, struggling though long days to make them stay on track, listening to my boss tell me all the things I could have been doing better, feeling like every solved problem just led to new problems - when all of that finally paid off with starting a new project, seeing easily where the problems could be, and offering little adjustments to make them go well. Someone might have watched me and said I made it look easy. It was gratifying when it happened. If only they knew how much hard work went into it.

By the time we all stood up from the table I felt I had recovered some pride. Getting lost in Wiedlin Meadows? Not so important. Nor was locking my keys in the car. Nor was dropping my badge on the ground the first time, nor the second. In the greater scheme of things, these were only nuisances, and, if I could be permitted to say so, I had handled them composure, good humor, and even dignity. Yes sir.

I led the way out of the room at the front of the other members of the team. It was time to go home after a productive day's work. I proceeded to the hallway door, exchanging a few pleasant remarks with the others walking behind me. Going to your son's soccer game tonight? Excellent. Just bought a new car? Wonderful - I'll bet it's a joy to drive.

That's how I imagined myself walking all the way to the front door: pleasant, calm, and in control.

"Mr. Close?" It was Jodie. She stood inside her cubicle as I was about to pass.

I turned to look at her. "Yes?" I answered, all gentility.

She smiled brightly. "Could you come in here for just a moment? I have just a couple more forms for you to fill out. It should only take a minute."

"Sure thing," I said. I turned back to the others and said, "Have a good evening, gentlemen. Thanks for all your hard work." It's always a good practice to acknowledge the hard work of others. They said goodbye and I took a seat in the guest chair next to Jodie.

She reached over to the stack of papers on the other side of her desk and set it down in front of me. She opened the pages of each document and drew X's and circles with her pen where I supposed to add my name and today's date. By the time she was done there weren't a couple forms to fill out, there were five or six, each requiring at least two signatures.

Well that's fine. There's always plenty of paperwork when you start a new engagement and this was no exception. I started signing and dating, resolved to complete it all without complaint.

Sign, date, sign, date, sign, date. It was all going fine except for the fact that I had forgotten today's date. It wasn't the 23rd of the month, like I was signing. It was the 22nd. I realized the mistake after I had signed them all and decided to ignore it. What difference did it make whether I agreed in writing to comply with Rejoice policies starting today or tomorrow?

Jodie, who checked my work on each page once I had finished it all, did not see it the same way. "Is that a 22 or a 23?" she asked.

Trying to be funny and make light of the mistake, answered, "Well, I guess it's a 22 now." I smiled.

Jodie smiled back at me and picked up a pen without looking at her desk. "Then you wouldn't mind if I changed the date and had you initial it?"

I realized I had made a mistake. Joking about being imprecise with a client's internal documents might not have seemed as funny to her as it did to me, especially since it was her job to make sure the documents were accurate. "No, ma'am, I wouldn't mind."

"Okay, I need your initials here...here...and here."

I initialed where she indicated. I was at the end of a long day and at the mercy of an administrative process whose importance I could not deny unless I wanted to make things even worse.

"You've had a hard day, haven't you?" Jodie said.

I looked up and laughed. "Yes, ma'am, I have." I thought I was better than that at hiding it. People in my position are supposed to be able to take bad news and long days without letting it bother them. This was a skill I had admired in other more experienced managers and one I had been working to develop in myself. Maybe I would be good at it eventually, but today all I wanted to do was get home to my wife so I could lay my head in her lap.

"It'll be easier next time," Jodie said. "Initial here, please."

"Yes, ma'am, it probably will." I initialed.

"You're all done," she said. "Thank you very much."

I stood up. "Thank you. See you next time."

I was free. Or at least I was if I could get out of the building. I counted myself lucky that I had to double back only twice before I found the front door.

As soon as I exited I called Kathy. "I'm coming home," I told her.

"Good! Why did it take so long? You were supposed to come home a couple hours ago."

"It's a long story, sweetie. I'll tell you when I get there."

She sounded skeptical. "Okay. Drive carefully."

"Oh I will. Don't you worry about that." Very carefully. We middle managers know the value of being careful.

After You

"We already agreed I'm going to die first," Kathy said to me.

Don't ask me how the subject of dying came up. It just does sometimes, and here it was again. It was Sunday morning and we were having breakfast after having slept in. Yes, I knew we had agreed a long time ago that she could go first, but that didn't mean I had to say so now. What fun would that be?

"I don't think so. Who's going to clean the house?" I asked.

"Maybe you'll learn to clean it," she said. "That's my theory."

I shook my head. "By the time you die I will be too old and frail for serious housework. The arthritis will keep me from holding a duster."

"Oh, please. A duster is very, very light."

"Not if your joints are all swollen." I put down my toast and rubbed my elbow the way I had seen people in ointment commercials do it. I winced to show her the pain.

Kathy rolled her eyes. "You might not be that old. For all we know I might go a lot sooner."

"True," I said. "True. And that's why I would like you to sign this life insurance policy." I slid an imaginary piece of paper over the table to her and offered an invisible pen. "If you kick the bucket, someone's-a-gonna be rich!"

"Oh, speaking of which," Kathy said, "did you move the money to the other account like I asked you yesterday?"

The pen and paper disappeared from the table. "No, I forgot."

"You'll do that today? I have bills to pay."

"Yes."

"Good."

Kathy took another bite of scrambled eggs, and so did I. I love breakfast food, especially on Sunday. A lot of hens have laid a lot of eggs so I could have moments like these.

"It doesn't matter when I go anyway," she said. "You'll still find another wife and she'll do all the housework, and she'll be twenty-two and spend eight hours a day at the health club."

"You really think so?" I had visions of a muscle-toned aerobics instructor holding a broom and dustpan, and honestly, I wasn't sure which part thrilled me more. Then I turned more serious. "I mean, noooo, no, never. It's you and me all the way to the end."

"Yeah, right," she said. "You know you have something all those girls want."

"I do? What?" I asked, although I was pretty sure I knew the answer.

"You have...a job," she said. "It takes a lot of money to keep her looking that good."

"Oh," I said. I had guessed wrong. "Is that why you stay with me? Because I have a job?"

"No, it's because I love wiping the water you leave all around the sink and helping you remember things I told you five minutes ago."

"I didn't forget those things," I said.

"Yes you did, and you didn't have a job when I moved in with you, remember?"

It was true: I didn't have a job. I had had one for almost five years running before that, but, almost like magic, I lost it a month before she moved halfway across the country to live with me. Funny how timing works out, isn't it?

"Finding a job is hard," I said. And it was - for me.

"I had one in two weeks." And she did. Her suitcases weren't even unpacked. Well, actually they were. Mine would have sat in the corner unpacked because I had other very important things to do, but hers were neatly unpacked after the first day.

"Could you vacuum the upstairs today?" she asked me.

"Sure, after my show is over." I always watch the Sunday political talk shows.

"I know," she said.

There was a moment of silence filled partially by the crunching of toast and sipping of coffee. Kathy checked her eBay page to see if she had sold anything in the last five minutes (she hadn't) and I looked down at our dog Jack, who, even though he had been blind for a year, was looking up at my toast.

"You know," I said, "if I die first, you could remarry, to the pool boy or someone like that."

"Nah," she said. "I got married once. That was enough."

"Oh, pooooooool boy, come over here..." I sing-songed.

"I can have him any time I want. I don't have to be married for that."

"True, but you do have to be married to get an artist-made teddy bear for your birthday, don't you?" I was referring to the bear dressed in waistcoat and spectacles sitting on a shelf upstairs.

"The pool boy wouldn't do it, but I bet Kevin at the grocery store would."

"Ah," I said. "Would he let you take it out of the box right away even though we bought it four months before your birthday?"

She pretended to think about this. "Yes," she answered. "Yes, he would."

"Oh," I said. "And he delivers the groceries. Sounds like he has the complete package."

"Mostly, but he doesn't have life insurance like you."

"What do you care whether I have insurance if you're going first?"

"Did I say that? No, what I meant is *you're* going first if you don't mow the lawn like you promised last week."

"Oh," I said. Seems like I say oh a lot.

"*That's* what I meant."

"Oh," I said again. "And what will you be doing?"

"Bringing you refreshing drinks so you don't dehydrate." She smiled up at me.

"Oh, sweetie..."

"So you can buy me another bear."

"Ah," I said. "Don't count on it. I'm saving up for a nursing home."

"You have plenty of time for that after you get the bear," she said. "He's dressed like a sailor and he's very cute."

"Do you have any idea how much nursing home care costs?"

"No, they're just going to pull the plug on me anyway. Why worry?"

"Not me," I said. "I'm gonna be strapped to a bed for a long time and it ain't gonna be cheap. The only reason I'm buying you all that stuff now is so I can auction it off for round-the-clock medical attention at the end of my life."

"Oh," she said. I could see her thinking of her collection disappearing and being replaced by steel aquamarine-colored breathing and peeing machines. It didn't make her face look any prettier, and that made me laugh out loud.

"Oh, stop it. That sounds awful," she said. "You should have them unplug you too. Maybe they could do us together." She put her hand on mine, and I have to admit it was kind of romantic. *Pop-pop* go our plugs.

But I reconsidered and shook my head. "Nah. By the time I want them to do it, I won't be able to ask."

"You could write them a note."

"Have you tried to read my handwriting? If it's bad now, just picture it when I'm old."

"I don't have to imagine it. Remember I met you by writing letters? I could barely read them. I must have been desperate." She sighed, "'Well, if he's a man and he can lick a stamp, who cares what he says.'"

"That's so sweet! And I said, 'I don't care if she lives six states over and runs the vacuum cleaner four times a day, she's the one for me.'"

"Speaking of cleaning," she began...

"Oh, God," I said. Cleaning again...

"Speaking of cleaning, I have to go sweep the basement. Could you clean up the plates and napkins from the table?"

"What do you think?"

"Well, I think you'll try and you'll get toast crumbs everywhere, and I'll praise you for it anyway."

"That's exactly right," I said, and I held out my hand for her napkin.

She blew her nose in it, balled it up and handed it to me. "Thank-you," she said.

She rose from her chair and went to the door to the steps leading down to the basement. She didn't have to bring the broom because she already keeps one on each floor of the house, and another one in the garage. She shut the basement door behind her - we don't want our blind dog going down there.

Then I heard a loud thumping sound and Kathy cry out, "Son of a bitch!"

I jumped up and flung the door open. "What happened?"

Kathy stood halfway down the stairs with both hands on the handrail. Her face was flush and there was a sheen of sweat on her forehead. "Tripped on a nail on the steps."

"You okay?"

She stood up straight. "Yeah, I'm fine. Get me the hammer, please."

I brought her the hammer and there followed a flurry of loud and opinionated banging on the subject of nails that stick up and trip people. When she handed the hammer back to me it was warm.

"Love you, sweetie," I said.

"Love you too," she answered, and I noticed that even with the nail flattened she still held onto the rail with one hand.

Unlimited

1: Football

My career as a student athlete was not impressive, but I remember moments of it even after twenty-five years. Between fifth and seventh grade I played football, basketball, and wrestled, and then I gave up sports and did not go back.

I discovered football in the fifth grade, the year the Oakland Raiders won the Super Bowl. The Raiders were my favorite team, as they had been ever since I saw them play on our old black and white television. The Raiders had great teams in those days. Those were the teams of John Madden, Ken Stabler, Cliff Branch, Fred Biletnikoff, Dave Casper, Mark van Eeghen, Ted Hendricks, and Ray Guy.

I was obsessed with the Raiders. I watched every game broadcast on NBC, and even after we got a color TV the Raiders still wore black. Every victory meant a good day and every defeat brought fierce disappointment. Looking back I can see now I would not have wanted to be my mother on a losing Sunday. Picture a scowling, stomping, huffing, non-answering young man carrying a football. If anyone deserved to have his head held under a tub of cold water after his team missed a field goal, it was me.

But there were joys as well as disappointments. For one, the Raiders won more than they lost, and even though the Denver Broncos kept them from the Super Bowl that year, it was a good season and better ones were still to come.

I started playing football myself at about that time. Or maybe I should say I played *with* the football. My parents bought me a ball and I threw it around inside and outside the house. My favorite game was to toss the ball so that I could make a fingertip catch and land on my bed. The harder the catch, the better. It just so happened that my bed was in the end zone, and I caught a lot of touchdown passes there.

I played catch with my dad whenever I could drag him into the street in front of our house. Dad stood beside our car and I stood beside our neighbor's car fifty feet away. We threw the ball, stopping only to avoid passing cars, until Dad's arm gave out and he decided he was done. My arm turned sore too, so that every throw hurt, but I did not care because the Spirit of Football had entered my body. It commanded me to throw the ball day and night and helped me through the pain.

I watched and played so much football, with friends, with my father, and by myself that my parents offered to sign me up for the YMCA flag football league. Play real football? On a team? "Hell yes!" I said. Why hadn't someone asked me sooner?

The team assembled at Comstock Park, located six blocks up Post Street from my house. I walked past the giant swimming pool, already emptied until next summer, and past the swing sets, where I might have liked to swing if I weren't about to join a football team. Football players don't swing. I walked through pine trees and emerged into the wide grassy field where other boys had already assembled, some playing catch with white-striped footballs. A man with a clipboard stood beside them. He looked old at the time, and I wouldn't realize until later that he was not so old, perhaps twenty.

I asked the man if this was the YMCA league and he said it was. I took my place among the others and soon the coach called for our attention.

He said his name was Kent, and he started out the practice by lining us up into rows and putting us through calisthenics: jumping jacks, pushups, and mountain climbers. Then he called us back together for football drills. First he split us into teams and had us run sprint relays using the football as the baton. He had us all run out for passes, where he threw the ball as we moved laterally across the field. I watched as some boys caught the passes and others didn't. He made each of us throw passes to him.

It was clear just from these few drills that some of the boys were faster than others, some had better hands for catching a football, and some could throw it better. I was somewhere in the middle of most of these measures, except the running. I was below average there. My big legs did not move fast and I ran out of breath easily.

A boy named Brett was the fastest runner. During the relay drill he ran in a straight line to the other end of the field and ran in a straight line back to the rest of us. His arms and knees pumped straight up and down and he ran straight and fast, the way a carpenter draws a grease pencil line on a piece of wood.

The ninety minutes went by quickly, and at the end he called us back together around him. "Okay guys. Good practice. Next time I'll have some teams drawn up so that you can see what position you're all playing. Be back here on time this Wednesday."

I walked home, tired but feeling good.

At the beginning of the next practice, Kent read from his clipboard. "Okay - Riley, you're playing quarterback, Brett, you're a halfback. Billy, you're halfback. John and Todd, you're receivers. Matt, you're our center. Charlie and Bob, you're guards..."

I stopped listening. Guard? I didn't know anything about playing guard. I had never played a game with a guard in it because it's a boring position that doesn't do anything. How many passes does a guard throw or catch? None. How many yards does he carry the ball? None. When I thought about football I didn't think about blocking.

But what could I do? I wanted to play football didn't I? I thought about quitting and going back to play catch in the street, but I didn't. I stuck to my position and tried to play it.

Years later I met David Diaz-Infante, who had played guard for the Denver Broncos. He was a friend of the president of the company where I worked at the time and he came to give a talk at a company meeting. He spoke about being undersized for an offensive lineman in the NFL at 6'3" and 295 lb., and how coaches overlooked him. He had had to earn a place on the team roster by working hard, having a positive attitude, and trying to prove to people that his ability to play was more important than his size. He told us how, even when he had impressed the coaches, he was usually cut from the team and sent to try out at the next team down the road. He said he had finally found a home with the Broncos, a team that had been good for years but had never been champions.

That changed in 1998 when, led by quarterback John Elway, the Broncos beat the Green Bay Packers to win Super Bowl XXXII. The sports pundits on TV agreed that Denver's secret strength was its offensive line which, although it was made up of smaller-than-average players, dominated the line of scrimmage.

I was impressed with David's talk. He showed us that working hard is as important as having talent and that persistence and confidence bring rewards. The president of my company wanted to make a connection between David and the company. Our company was small and trying to outperform some big, wealthy competitors. David's example showed us that if we were disciplined, committed, and played as a team, we could succeed.

When he started talking he did something even better than the talk itself. He pulled his Super Bowl ring off his hand and gave it to us to pass around while he was speaking. I may have been a grown man who was not easily impressed but I was impressed by that. First of all, it was a Super Bowl ring. I had seen them on television on the hands of coaches or broadcasters, but I had never seen one in person. Second, if I had a trophy like that I'm not sure I'd be able to take it out of the trophy case at home much less pass it around to a room full of strangers. What if someone lost it or stole it? What if someone dropped it and knocked out one of the diamonds? If I passed *my* ring around I'd spend a lot less time talking and a lot more time watching it.

Not Dave. He started the ring off at one end of the room and kept on talking about all the camps he had been turned away from before he arrived in Denver. Meanwhile the ring circulated. It was easy to follow its progress by watching the moving cluster of bowed heads.

I sat on the side of the room opposite from where it started, so I was one of the last people to see the ring. The person who handed it to me met my eyes. It was a meaningful moment that seemed to say, *"With this hand I do pass unto thee the ring of the Super Bowl. Bestow ye upon it great care, good and worthy sir."* Or maybe it said, "Holy crap! Can you believe this? It's a friggin' Super Bowl ring."

In return my look communicated, *"Fear not. I shall give unto the last beat of my heart to keep intact that which you have entrusted to me."* Or maybe it said, "C'mon, c'mon, give it, ring hog!" Either way, we understood each other. He gave it to me and my head bowed.

The thing to understand about Super Bowl rings, and I can say this with some authority, is that they should not be judged by the usual standards. A Super Bowl ring is a trophy first and a piece of jewelry second. As a trophy it was fabulous. The ring was huge and probably weighed a couple of ounces. The band was very wide and came to a flat top. It was etched on all sides with different numbers and symbols, like the year, and "XXXII", and the score of the game, 31-24. Every feature of the ring had significance. Dave explained them to us as part of his talk. "Each diamond symbolizes a different player on the team..." That kind of thing.

As a piece of jewelry it was less impressive. Think of it like a class ring only ten times as much. It was big, heavy, gaudy, and not even a little subtle. The flat top was so wide that if it had been the pope's ring, two people could have kissed it at the same time.

It didn't matter how flashy it was. It was a Super Bowl ring, a talisman of the Spirit of Football. Maybe the Spirit wasn't as strong in me as it had been when I was a boy, but when I handed it to the next person I did so with almost ritual solemnity. It might be a long time before I saw another one of these.

And, in a corner of my mind that I am not proud of, I thought, "That is probably the closest I will ever come to seeing John Elway's Super Bowl ring."

Playing guard did not come easily for me. I had only one qualification: my size. I stood five-foot-three and weighed over a hundred pounds - big for a fifth-grader. Other than that I had a lot to learn. Playing guard, it helps to be strong, and I was not strong, and it helps to be fast and aggressive, which I was not.

If I were eleven years old today, what with modern advances in athletic training, and a culture that tries to make old people young and young people old, I would probably have spent a lot of time in the weight room. I would have worked to develop that bulging triangle of muscle on each shoulder and a six pack on my stomach, and, as a student athlete, I would have done this while maintaining good grades in spelling, penmanship, and fractions.

But I was eleven a quarter century ago and I made do with the body and skills I had. It turns out that playing guard is harder than it looks on television. To the untrained eye the line of scrimmage looks like a grinding, squeezing pile of people accomplishing nothing. The only action emerging from the pile is when a defensive player breaks free from it and tries to sack the quarterback.

Even though it seems obvious, what I didn't appreciate at the time is that the offensive line is the only thing that keeps the defensive line from sacking the quarterback on every play.

If it weren't for the offensive line there would be no running plays, no passing plays, and the quarterback would have to snap the ball from his own butt. The job of a guard is critical even if it not glamorous.

The other hard thing about playing guard was that I wasn't expected just to block the defenders from the quarterback: I had to push them in a particular direction. I was amazed. It wasn't enough to stop the defender. I was supposed to move him four feet to the left, away from the running backs. If offensive linemen on TV did this, I never noticed it from looking at the throbbing pile.

Kent kept the offense simple. Young quarterbacks can't throw well and young receivers can't catch either, so we didn't run many passing plays. But our running backs! That was a different story. Brett and Billy could run around, through, and away from anyone. They were fast and strong and slippery, and they possessed other advantages. First, eleven year olds don't play as a team. Our backs could outmaneuver and outrun almost anyone, and the defense couldn't get organized enough to gang up on them. We gained thousands of yards on the ground, so much that we called the territory past the goal line the Brett Zone and we had a special play called First and Billy.

The other thing that helped our running backs is that we were playing flag football, not tackle.

For those who don't know how flag football works, it's just like tackle football except that it has no tackling. Every player wears a belt with a long strip of nylon attached by Velcro to each hip. A player with the ball is "tackled" by ripping off one of the flags.

The use of flags combines the best of both touch football and tackle football. It's non-violent like two-hand touch, and, like tackle, when the man with the ball is "down" you know it for sure.

Some may argue that the football flag is one of the most important technical inventions in all of sports, in the same class as shoulder pads in football and the shot clock in basketball. It allows boys to play team football at a younger age with less risk of injury.

Me, I'm not so sure. I've seen young boys play, and they *love* to hit and knock each other to the ground. Pound for pound, eleven year old boys are the most violent animals this side of a badger. They have no fear, and why would they? They think they can't be injured. Letting them play tackle makes all the sense in the world.

Adults know that bones can break, and that careers and even lives can end in a single play. A body can be knocked down only so many times before it starts to wear out, so that by the time a player reaches his twenties he thinks the game could cause lasting damage, and by the time he reaches his thirties he is sure it will.

That's why I think the adult players should use flags, not the kids. Picture this: a 200 pound running back, all muscle, breaking downfield with the football and charging for the end zone. His yellow flags flap in the wind made by his own speed. Coming at him, a massive linebacker with fierce eyes and dancing red flags. Who will win this battle of speed versus strength - the hunter or the hunted? This time the linebacker wins. He charges into the running back's path and rips off his flag. The back stops and the play is over. The linebacker, triumphant, whirls the flag in the air and performs a wobbly-kneed taunt walk for the roaring crowd.

Others may laugh, but I think this would greatly improve pro football.

Playing with flags helped Billy and Brett because it emphasized speed and limberness over strength. They were so fast that no defender could outrun them, and if a defender ever got close, they could swish and twist the flags out of reach. They were unstoppable. The referees came home every Saturday with tired arms from holding them up in the touchdown position. Even though I wasn't playing quarterback or wide receiver like I wanted to, it still felt good to play for a winning team.

There were other joys as well. We got our uniforms early in the season. Kent bent over a cardboard box with the top cut open, and those of us standing closest to it looked over the flaps and saw a soft pile of T-shirts. They were the whitest, cleanest shirts I had ever seen, and the navy blue lettering was as crisp as the early autumn air. The Spirit of Football ran powerfully through me at that moment. It shined out through my eyes.

Kent called out sizes and players stepped up. "Medium!" Billy came forward. "Large!" Danny walked forward. "Extra Large!" I walked up to the box and took the shirt that Kent teased out of it.

I walked back to the edge of the crowd and looked at my shirt. Not only did it have blue lettering, it also had long blue sleeves. Best of all, it had a big number on the back: 51. Only real football jerseys have a number, and this one did, and that meant I was a real football player.

The boys pulled off the shirts they came in and threw them down in piles. They lay scattered by a tree like dead leaves while they pulled on their new shirts, and a gang of young boys, transformed by the power of white cotton, turned into a football team.

I loved the flags too. We each pulled a belt from a rack before the start of every game and fastened the frayed end through the pair of steel loops of the other end. I looked down at my flags as I walked along the sidelines, and I tried to make them bounce without wiggling conspicuously. I wanted to twirl them, but I didn't because the other boys would see me. Out on the field I put my hands on my hips before dropping into a three point stance, and the flags flapped in the Saturday morning breeze like a dare to the defender in front of me.

The defender might step around me or push me to one side after the snap, but it didn't matter. For that moment before he passed me and ran screaming at our quarterback I was the incarnation of flag football, made manifest by the wearing of the flag belt. I could not have been any holier if I had been the Dalai Lama himself.

And neither could my blocking.

My experience with flag football, while it did not turn out the way I had hoped, taught me some valuable lessons. That is, it would have if I had been paying attention.

If I had been paying attention I would have learned that it is easy to imagine you are good at something but harder to become good at it in reality. I did not make the team as a quarterback or a receiver because, despite wanting to, I did not have the skills.

And if I had been paying attention I would have learned that even though I did not play the role I wanted to, the role I was given was still valuable. If I had been more grown up I would have brought more enthusiasm to playing on the offensive line, like David Diaz-Infante.

And, if I had been paying attention I would have appreciated that you can be bad at one thing but good at other things. This lesson seems so obvious, and yet it was hard to learn when I was getting my ass kicked at football.

For example, although I was a poor athlete I was a very good student. When I was eleven I read books well above grade level and my library card was creased and the corners were torn off from weekly use. My father was a geologist and my mother had returned to school to study biology and chemistry, so I was wise in the ways of science. In those days it seemed right and proper that I should share the gift of knowledge with my fifth grade class.

One day, the spring before that flag football season, the girls in my class were sent to another room and we boys stayed behind, restless with fear and excitement, to receive public school sex education. We watched a film about Joey, a much older boy of fourteen who was just beginning puberty, and we learned that his body was going through many changes that would seem confusing at first but were necessary for him to become a man. Perhaps the most shocking of these changes was that he had to shower every day, not just take a bath once a week like the rest of us. This seemed like a horrible waste of time.

My class watched the film without blinking, and when Mr. Marz turned the lights back on he described the details of human reproduction. The class sat still, half stunned.

But not I. I already knew it all because my mother had explained it to my brother and me while taking her first year college biology class. I had mastered all the facts.

Mr. Marz went over the high points and tried to start a discussion. He asked questions, looking for response from the class.

I was ready. Mr. Marz had hardly finished his question before my hand shot up.

"Sperm!" I shouted. I didn't wait for him to call on me.

It was the beginning of an afternoon in which my education unfolded into full view. I knew all about eggs, sperm, the uterus, fallopian tubes, and the vas deferens. My only regret was that the girls were not present to see me at my best.

2: Basketball

I played basketball the next year, a sport I knew even less about than football. My only useful skill as a player was that I was tall.

I played horse in the back yard with my father and my brother, so I could shoot. In real games, however, there are five players on a team, not just one, and, unlike horse, everyone runs all the time. And I hated running.

I played on both the school team and a YMCA team. Mr. Wiley coached the sixth grade team and my father coached for the Y.

Because I was tall, I was assigned the position of forward. I did not know what a forward was supposed to do, but I learned early on that the team's offensive system was not built around having the forwards shoot the ball. The other players, who I learned later were called guards, took all the shots.

The only basketball I knew was horse. If I wasn't supposed to shoot the ball, what was I supposed to do? And *hey!* What was it about foot*ball* and basket*ball* that meant I wasn't supposed to touch the ball?

My father explained that the forward's job is to stay close to the basket and get rebounds.

"What's a rebound?" I asked. I really didn't know very much about basketball.

Dad told me that when a player misses a shot, the loose ball is called a rebound, and a forward's job is to get them so that his team can go on offense.

I thought, okay, fine. It seemed to me that playing forward on a basketball team is a lot like playing guard on a football team - no glory. It was nothing at all like knowing what a urethra is on sex education day.

So I obeyed the letter of my father's advice but not the spirit. In the words of Charles Barkley, one of the best forwards who ever played, Dad wanted me to put some ass on my opponent - get up on him, slow him down, make him think, and make him work. My other job, again quoting Barkley, was to get the damn ball. When I was twelve I did not understand that if I was the kind of player who could put some ass on somebody and get the damn ball I could help my team win as much as the players taking the shots.

Instead of doing what Dad wanted, but didn't ask for, I spent most of the time directly under the rim of the basket, waiting flat-footed for gravity to bring the ball to shoulder level where I could catch it. The funny thing about the spot under the rim is that rebounds don't go there, only made baskets. Rebounds bounce away from the rim, where other players waited in a better position to grab them. It didn't seem fair that I should do what I was told and I still didn't get to touch the ball.

The YMCA league that my dad coached mostly consisted of boys, but there were a few girls, and some of them played as hard as any boy. I remember a game where one girl on the other team played harder than all the other nine players on the court. In one play a teammate of hers passed the ball too hard and it was about to go out of bounds near the basket, and this girl ran the ball down, leaped in the air and spanked the ball back inbounds before landing out of bounds herself. By doing this she kept the ball in play so that her team would have a chance to catch it and score.

I had never seen a play like it before. I stopped running and looked at Dad on the sidelines. My look said, "She can't do that!"

Dad waved his hands for me to keep playing. "Go! Go!"

I shook my head and jogged back to my place under the rim.

Dad faced his share of challenges even without me as a player. One Saturday only five of our players showed up, just enough to put a team on the floor. Every player on our team would have to play the whole game without rest. The other team, it so happened, had fifteen players. They had twice as many reserves as we had starters!

Oh, I'm sure it wasn't easy for the other team. Managing egos must have been hard, what with the number thirteen, fourteen, and fifteen players relaying notes to the coach to ask for more playing time. I looked at the players at the far end of the bench, not scoring any baskets and little chance that they would. They were, I was sure, all forwards.

My father, faced with three-to-one odds, huddled us all together. He looked us in the eye and said, "I want you to go out there and wear them down."

My experience with the grade school team wasn't any better. Two memories stand out.

The first thing was the different drills we practiced to improve our passing and moving without the ball. The one I remember was drill #2. We started with each of us standing at a point on the floor. We were supposed to catch the ball, pass it to the next player, and rotate to a new spot on the floor. It should have been simple: catch-pass-move, catch-pass-move.

It was not simple for me. I could never figure out when the ball was coming to me, or who to pass it to, or where to go next. Balls bounced off the side of my head when I wasn't looking, and I was always in the path of the boy running to take my spot, or caught in no-man's land between where I had been and where I was supposed to go. I wish the drill had been caught on video from the gym ceiling. I have no doubt that it would show four players moving in a circle to the right and one player staggering to the left. How I survived a single practice, much less a whole season, remains a mystery to me.

The other event I remember came after one especially hard practice. We sweating boys stood in a circle around Mr. Wiley.

"You all worked hard today. I'm going to send for some sodas so you can cool off. Just tell me what you want." Mr. Wiley flipped a clean sheet over his clipboard and pulled out a pen.

He called us by last name.

"Jones?" he said.

"Orange."

"Ridgeley?"

"Orange."

"Close?"

"Grape," I said.

Mr. Wiley continued down the list and every single player except me wanted orange soda.

"Well," said Mr. Wiley, "I've got nine orange sodas and one big grape for Good Time Charlie."

Just me? Grape? Good Time Charlie? I felt conspicuous and I did not like to feel conspicuous. "Um, I'll have orange too," I said.

Mr. Wiley made a note on his clipboard. "Good Time Charlie wants orange. Orange it is. I'll be back in five minutes."

The funny thing is, I don't remember a single shot, rebound, pass, steal, or block I made on that team, but even now I wish I had stuck with grape.

Playing basketball taught me lessons that I did not notice at the time.

If I had been paying attention I would have learned that enthusiasm and intensity count as much as skill. Or I would have learned to like the things I like, like grape soda, and let others like the things they like.

But no, my brain remained impenetrable. I didn't learn anything from sports that year.

Not to worry. Mr. Wiley was my sixth grade teacher. As dire as things were on his basketball court, I still shone in his classroom.

Mr. Wiley liked to reward students who spoke up in class. Any time a student answered a question correctly, he sent them to put their initials in the corner of the blackboard. A boy or girl was allowed to make up to five trips to the board each day, and each day Mr. Wiley added the blackboard points to the total that made up their quarterly grade.

My hand was up *all* the time. I wore out three pairs of Oxford dress shoes that year strutting up to the front of the room to write "CC".

Mr. Wiley also liked to help his students build their vocabulary. He required students to learn three new words each week, write them on recipe cards, and bring them to his desk for a small one-on-one quiz.

I loved vocabulary, and it so happened that I loved biochemistry too. Mom had been studying it and some of it had rubbed off on me. The first time I walked to Mr. Wiley's desk with the cards in my hand I was ready.

He looked at the first one. It said "dextrose".

He flipped to the second, which said "sucrose".

I waited for him to look at the third: "glucose". I smiled sweetly.

"What kinds of words are those?" he asked.

"Those are all varieties of sugar," I answered. Duh.

He folded the cards and handed them back to me. "That's fine for this week, but next week I want you to try some normal words."

I went back to my desk in a sour mood, but not for long. Later that year I offered to give a talk about the theory of relativity to the class. I told Mr. Wiley that I would like to give a presentation on the meaning of the most famous equation in the history of science: $E = mc^2$.

Mr. Wiley accepted. Later that week I stood before the class in front of the blackboard with a piece of chalk in my hand.

The talk did not go the way I wanted. I had not prepared as well as I should have, and I did not know as much about relativity as I thought I did. My classmates, who I had assumed would be fascinated and impressed, stared at me and were silent.

My presentation on Einsteinian physics began to unravel as soon as it started. I spoke too quickly, and the seconds passed very, very slowly. In the end I took half as much time as I had been allotted and sat back down, humbled. To add insult to injury, we used the leftover time on fractions.

Despite a few setbacks, that year marked the height of my academic achievement. I have never been so smart since, even though I never did figure out drill #2.

3: Wrestling

I started the seventh grade the next year and turned out for the wrestling team.

Let me say at the outset that this was my last and worst experience with team sports.

The wrestling team was coached by Mr. Ensign, my home room teacher and a veteran of the Korean War. He looked it, too. He was five-foot-nine, four feet wide and ninety-eight percent muscle. His crew cut had turned mostly gray and he spoke in words of no more than one syllable. For him, doors were only a convenience. Had he chosen to do so, he could have left any room at any time through the flat part of the wall.

Wrestling was not a good sport for me for two reasons. The first was the practices. Wrestling was even more physically demanding than football and basketball had been. For a sport that takes place on a circle only a few feet wide there is an awful lot of running involved. I ran hundreds of sprints back and forth across the width of the gym, and thousands of laps around its perimeter, and I ran more miles standing in place next to my fellow wrestlers – knees up, knees up, knees up!

Running was the easy part. There were also push ups, pull ups, chin ups, and sit ups. We practiced lying on our backs on the wrestling mat and, at the sound of the whistle, flipping fast onto our stomachs, over and over.

You have to love wrestling to be in wrestling. It is the hardest, sweatiest, grossest sport of them all. Wrestlers spend hours sweating and gripping each other in a hot damp room, and they spit gallons of spit into water fountains to lose weight, or drink gallons of water from those same fountains to gain it.

To make it worse, that was the year when I reached the age of thirteen, almost the same age as Joey in the fifth grade sex education film, and sure enough, I had to shower every day.

Put it all together and wrestling was too much for me. It was too physically strenuous and it wasn't fun. So I started skipping practices.

Mr. Ensign confronted me before homeroom after the third absence.

"You weren't at practice last night. Where were you?"

"I don't know," I said.

"Were you sick?"

"No, I was busy."

"Busy with what?"

"Homework." I thought that was a good answer. How could he blame me for wanting to do well in my classes?

"Do your homework after practice."

"I can't."

"Why?"

I shrugged. "I don't have the time."

He folded his arms over his chest. They were thick, hairy, and graying. Men like this had won the Cold War. "How many hours do you have?"

"What?" I asked.

"How many hours do you have in a day?"

I had no idea what he wanted. "Twenty-four?"

"Right. Twenty-four."

I said nothing. I still didn't understand.

"Twenty-four," he said. "Just like everyone else. Just like your team. They do their homework. They come to practice every day. Why can't you?"

"I don't know," I said.

"I don't either. And I don't care. You want to quit, then quit. If you are going to stay, then stay. Just don't waste our time. Get it?"

I nodded.

"Good. Practice tonight, same time."

I did not quit, although I probably should have. I had only one skill as a wrestler: I was heavy. I was one of the heaviest thirteen-year-olds in the school. Unfortunately I did not have strength in proportion to my size, nor did I have catlike quickness. I had the soulful eyes and soft physique of a hound dog.

Furthermore, wrestling is designed to minimize the advantage of extra weight. Wrestlers are segregated into weight classes of just a few pounds difference. Everyone you wrestle weighs no more than seven pounds more or less than you

One of the skills of the sport is to stay at the heavy end of your best weight class to get the maximum advantage over your opponent. Staying at the right weight takes focus and determination as well as a merciless attention to ounces of water going into the body or coming out. That's why wrestlers who needed to lose weight before a match spent time running and spitting and wrestlers who needed to gain weight drank so much.

For us seventh-graders the second to last weight class was 155 pounds, and the last was called Unlimited. Unlimited was where they stopped counting. It didn't matter if you weighed 162 or 362. Let the wrestling begin! I wrestled in the Unlimited class, but I was not blessed with 300 pounds of wrestling weight.

Mr. Ensign worked to prepare us for our wrestling matches. He drilled us hard and he showed us new holds and moves. Sometimes he demonstrated them personally.

He stood in front of us in heavy gray sweat pants and sweat jacket. He called, "Peterson, up here!"

Mike Peterson walked to the front and Mr. Ensign put his hand on Mike's shoulder. He said to the team, "I'm going to show you this. Learned it in the war."

Then Mr. Ensign did something - I'm not sure what - and Mike was flat on his back with his legs sticking out at different angles.

Mr. Ensign said, "See that?" We all nodded. Mike, most of whose face was obscured by Mr. Ensign's thigh, nodded too.

"Good. Let's practice it."

The practices were the first bad thing about wrestling. The second was the wrestling meets against other schools.

I did not win many of my matches. Most of the other schools had wrestlers in the Unlimited class who could loosen the bolts on a jet engine or castrate a bull with their bare hands. They were real athletes, not like me.

I tried. I pulled on my singlet and strapped on the aluminum earmuffs that kept my opponent from pulling my ears off. I like to think I looked pretty good. That is, until I stepped onto the mat with boys who were twice my size.

Imagine now that I am saying this while lying on my back with a large boy riding my chest: wrestling was not a good sport for me. *Ow.* I learned all about the two-second lifetime between the moment my shoulders hit the mat and when the referee slapped his hand by my ear, signaling that I had been pinned and the match was over. I got up after my opponent got up and we each walked back to our bench. I did not like having to look at my teammates. Sometimes they didn't look back at me.

But I did not lose all my matches. One week we wrestled against a cross-town rival and my opponent and I were evenly matched.

He was four inches shorter than I, and three inches wider. He wore a blue mesh jersey and I could see through it that he was soft like the inside of a lobster.

Before we started I looked at him and he looked at me. Both of us thought for the first time all season that we might win.

My opponent was worthy, but I was the better wrestler that day. Even though he was too squishy to pin, I scored a lot of points on him, and in the end I rose from the mat with the victory.

The score was 9 to 8.

That's a high score, like 15 to 14 in baseball or 45 to 42 in football. A score like that means that there was a lot of rolling around without going for the kill.

It didn't matter. I started to run off the mat back to the bench, ready to whoop out loud, but I stopped myself short and resumed a walk. Keep it cool. Keep it cool. When I looked at my teammates, they looked back. Whoa! Keep it cool.

That match was the last one of the year. The season ended and so did my career as a student athlete.

I learned lessons from wrestling, although of course I didn't know it then. I learned that you shouldn't commit to something half way. I shouldn't have been on the wrestling team at all, but as long as I was Mr. Ensign was right to expect me to show up, work hard, and try.

I also learned that almost anything you want to be good at requires doing things you don't like. One of the perks of wrestling in the Unlimited class was that I never had to spit into a drinking fountain to lose weight, but plenty of my teammates had to do it, and they did it.

I learned that the worst part about being bad at something in a group of other people who are good at it is that you don't feel like a part of the group. There is no worse feeling than knowing that you are the one who makes it worse for everyone else, and knowing that they know it too. I always felt alone at times like these, but the wrestler I beat showed me I was not alone.

And last, I accepted, although not until much later, that as ungifted as I was, as ungrateful as I was, as much as I could have and should have tried harder, I did sign up, I did show up, I did try, and I did get something from sports. I only wish that I had allowed myself to get more.

Even though I played team sports for the last time in the seventh grade, the climax of my school age love for football did not come until the next year.

That was the year that the Oakland Raiders played Super Bowl XV and beat the Philadelphia Eagles.

What could be better than that? I'll tell you what. The Super Bowl was on my birthday. I got to watch my favorite team win the Super Bowl while eating birthday cake.

And even that wasn't all. It got better. My parents got me my own electric typewriter, a used IBM Selectric, the best typewriter ever made. I have worked on many keyboards since, and nothing has improved on its touch, speed, and sound. The Selectric was the Steinway of office equipment.

This was not a small gift for a fourteen year old boy. It cost $400, a lot of money in those days.

I did not waste that gift. I used it for all my schoolwork until I left for college. I even wrote a novel on it. I wrote a page almost every day for thirteen months, and in the end I had a 476-page book. It was a fantasy novel about a man from our world whose wedding ring had magic powers in a fantasy world. He was summoned to the other world by the members of a wise council who enlisted him to use his magic ring to fight the emperor of darkness. He did, reluctantly, and eventually the evil was destroyed.

The end of the novel even featured a chess game between the hero and the emperor. I had discovered chess about that time and got the idea of playing against evil from a music video by the band Kansas. Lousy song, but great concept.

It was the most horrible, derivative novel ever written. I had just finished reading *The Chronicles of Thomas Covenant* by Stephen R. Donaldson for the third time and was driven to write something that would inspire others the way those books had inspired me. I didn't do a single thing that Donaldson, and his own forbearer, J.R.R. Tolkien, didn't do much better and years earlier.

That said, it is still true that I wrote an entire novel at the age of fourteen, and I did it by working a little at a time for a long, long time. Just think what I might have accomplished if I had put the same consistent effort into blocking, rebounding, and wrestling holds.

4: Basketball Again

These days I still play sports a little bit. My wife's friend Wendy has a daughter named Kendall who loves sports. Soccer is her real game but she also likes to play basketball with her friends and me in her driveway.

Kendall is ten years old and she is small even for a girl her age, four-foot-eight and seventy-five pounds. I am a foot and a half taller and over two hundred pounds heavier, huge compared to her.

We've been playing for almost a year now, just horse at first. I could almost always outshoot her, and even when she would take the lead I could focus and make my shots while she started to choke. She could rarely maintain the calm needed to beat someone older like me when I got serious.

Like when my father played me, I never gave her a break. I looked for shots outside her comfort zone: hook shots, scoop shots, left-handed shots. The closer she came to beating me, the more I showed her my hard-to-do shots, and that almost always broke her down. She won a few games, but none of them as gimmies from me.

She complained at first. You're too tall! I can't make it from that far away! Please don't shoot a hook shot again, please! She used the only tool she thought she had, pleading for adult mercy.

I didn't listen. I wanted to win and if she was going to beat me she had to outplay me, which wasn't easy for her when I had all the physical advantages.

Eventually Kendall stopped complaining and started to play, and her shot improved. Now she can make lay-ups and ten-footers consistently, and I've even seen her score against her own friends with a hook shot.

Then she discovered how to shoot with her back to the basket and throw the ball two-handed back over her head. She is wickedly accurate with that shot. It's the stupidest shot ever and has no place at all in a real basketball game. It is, however, legal in her driveway, and I haven't made one yet, so when she is leading a game of horse she makes me take it ten times in a row. She plays to finish me off, and she has beaten me multiple times with it.

I wish my father could be there to see her. She does exactly what he would do.

We've also started playing one on one. I can block almost any shot she takes, but I have worked with her to show her how to dribble around me and create space to shoot. I've taught her that she needs to shoot fast before the defense closes in, and I demand that she not give up on the rebound when I get the ball close to the basket. Who knows, maybe I'll miss.

She does not plead anymore. Sometimes she yells in frustration at me for being so tall, but mostly she just plays.

Nowadays her father or her friends join us to play two-on-one against me. If I guard Kendall, she passes the ball to the open player and tells him to shoot. If I sag off her to guard the other player, she steps up to take the shot herself. She takes advantage of the fact that I can't be in two places at one time and she relies on her teammates to beat me.

I told her she should turn out for the school basketball team next year, and she said she's not good enough. I don't know if she believed her own words, or if she was just making sure she has enough time for soccer. I told her she is good enough and that we have all summer to work on her game, and I know I meant what I said.

Maybe wrestling is next, eh? Girls can do that these days.

Well, she should play with someone her own size for that. Chances are that if she ever turns out for wrestling Kendall won't be Unlimited like I was - you can't coach weight, after all. But it looks to me like she will be unlimited in her own way.

Printed in the United States
138302LV00001B/2/P